THE ART OF

WORLD BUILDING

WORKBOOK:

FANTASY EDITION

THE ART OF WORLD BUILDING SERIES

RANDY ELLEFSON

Evermore Press
GAITHERSBURG, MARYLAND

Evermore Press, LLC
Gaithersburg, Maryland
www.evermorepress.org

The Art of World Building Workbook: Fantasy Edition / Randy Ellefson. -- 1st ed.
ISBN 978-1-946995-52-0 (paperback)
ISBN 978-1-946995-54-4 (hardback)

Contents

ACKNOWLEDGEMENTS

Cover design by Randy Ellefson

INTRODUCTION

The Art of World Building Workbook is designed for storytellers, game designers, and hobbyists to create in-depth worlds that can help your work stand out from the considerable competition out there. The worksheets are the product of decades of world building expertise, research, and the authoring of *The Art of World Building* book series, podcast, blog and YouTube channel. The books include templates and examples of how to fill out many of them. Those templates have been turned into this workbook.

This workbook is intended to be used for a single project. A fantasy world builder in need of two *detailed* planets would need two workbooks, as the fantasy edition is arranged for one. For a sci-fi world builder, the scope is broader but less detailed – space to define multiple solar systems and planets is included here, each with fewer specifics; a project that sprawls to dozens of systems and planets would need additional workbooks.

THE WORKBOOK EDITIONS

The workbook comes in two editions: fantasy and sci-fi. Minor differences between them are throughout and do not require explanation. For example, the legal section might ask, "Are there laws about the use of magic?" vs. "Are there laws about the use of technology?" But other differences are significant and result in entire sections being added or removed, or reduced/increased in size and scope. For example, fantasy world builders don't typically need spacecraft, and the need for gods is reduced in sci-fi. All differences have a rationalization but are not explained here. The major differences are summarized in this table.

Section	Fantasy Edition	Sci-Fi Edition
Solar systems	Only one	Several
Planets	Only one	Several
World history	Detailed	Shortened and multiple worlds
Land features	Detailed	Shortened
Gods and pantheons	Detailed	Shortened
Magic systems and spells	Detailed	Shortened
Space craft, AI, and technology	Omitted	Included

By contrast, both editions include virtually identical sections on the universe/galaxy, land and sea features (including plants and animals), sovereign powers, settlements, places of interest, species/races, world figures, monsters, undead, cultures, organizations, armed forces, religions, the supernatural, items, names, games and sports, and legal, education, and monetary systems. When these subjects differ between genres, it is mostly in the number of worksheets/items you might need. For example, sci-fi often needs multiple solar systems but fantasy rarely does. The generalizations exist not to restrict the work you perform, but to avoid too many unneeded pages for most world builders. There is no ideal solution because project needs vary, and someone will inevitably be disappointed regardless of this book's layout. The book attempts to satisfy the needs of the greatest number of world builders. Those who need more sheets for a subject may wish to photocopy pages before filling them out.

THE ART OF WORLD BUILDING SERIES

In an effort to keep the length of this workbook no longer than needed, explanations and theories about world building are kept to a minimum. After all, there are three full volumes of in-depth analysis, guidance, and recommendations available. Having read the series is not necessary, however, as the world building prompts herein are self-explanatory. For those interested in advice, the volumes are summarized below so you know which one will help your areas of concern.

More books are available in the series, including two workbooks, all at Amazon: https://amzn.to/3y7mN1B

CREATING LIFE (VOLUME ONE)

Everything we need to know about how to create gods, species/races, plants, animals, monsters, heroes, villains, and undead is included in *Creating Life (The Art of World Building, #1)*. Some basic techniques are also discussed, such as using analogies and deciding how many worlds to build in a career.

CREATING PLACES (VOLUME TWO)

The life we create needs to originate from somewhere on a planet: an ocean, a continent, in a land feature (like a forest or mountain range), in a kingdom, or in a settlement. *Creating Places (The Art of World Building, #2)* goes into detail about inventing such locations and figuring out how long it takes to travel between them by various forms of locomotion: foot, horse, wagon, dragon, wooden ship, spaceship, and more. The overall rules of our world are also considered, along with inventing time, history, various places of interest, and how to draw maps. We can start our work with any one of those subjects and crisscross between places and life, for one often impacts the other.

CULTURES AND BEYOND (VOLUME THREE)

Everything not covered in the first two volumes lies in the finale, *Cultures and Beyond (The Art of World Building, #3)*. This includes creating culture, organizations, armed forces, religions, the supernatural, magic systems, technological and supernatural items, languages, names, and various systems our world will have, from health, educational, legal, commerce, to information systems. Finally, we look at how to manage our world building projects. Without these subjects, no world building project is complete.

WHERE TO START

World building can be done in any order, but it is recommended that before you begin, you flip through this entire book to gain a feel for its layout. There is some natural overlap and it can be good to understand and note where these occur. For example, for both legal systems and education systems, these are defined in later sections of the workbook. And once defined there, they can be referred to in both the sovereign powers and settlements sections. If apprenticeships are possible, we might define it in the education systems section and then note the existence, or lack thereof, of apprenticeships in a city or kingdom we are inventing. Monetary systems are also used this way, for while variation can occur at regional levels, some versions might be nearly universal and are better defined in a central location in this workbook, namely the monetary systems section. This is also true of games and sports, which can transcend locale.

Cultures may be regional or not. For example, on Earth, jocks might be mostly the same regardless of origin, but everyone (including jocks) from the southeast of a continent might also share a culture. In this book series, this is known as cultural scope, meaning we should define what we're creating culture for – a country, region, city, or social group, as examples.

This book is organized in a top-down approach, meaning universe, planet, continent, sovereign power, and down to settlement, for example. However, it doesn't need to be filled out in that order. But given that the broader scale affects the smaller scale in real life, it seems a sensible organization, at the least. *The Art of World Building* book series is ordered similarly.

About Me

By profession I'm a software developer, but I've been writing fantasy fiction since 1988 and building worlds just as long, mostly one planet called Llurien. Yes, I am crazy. But I love what I do. I didn't intend to work on it for so long, but when life has prevented me from writing, I've worked on Llurien. I've done everything in these chapters and authored two hundred thousand words of world building in my files. Llurien even has a website at www.llurien.com. I've written six novels and over a dozen short stories over the years, and have just begun my publishing career with a novella that you can read for free (see below).

I'm also a musician with a degree in classical guitar; I've released three albums of instrumental rock, one classical guitar CD, and a disc of acoustic guitar instrumentals. You can learn more, hear songs, and see videos at my main website, http://www.randyellefson.com.

Free Book

If you'd like to see a sample of my world building efforts in action, anyone who joins my fiction newsletter mailing list receives a free eBook of *The Ever Fiend (Talon Stormbringer)*. Please note there's also a separate newsletter for *The Art of World Building*, though both can be joined on the same signup form. Just check the box for each.

WORLD BUILDING UNIVERSITY

World Building University (WBU) has online courses that provide step-by-step instruction on creating all aspects of great fantasy and science fiction worlds. Each includes a series of video lessons, quizzes to test your retention of what you've learned, and assignments designed to make your creation a reality instead of a dream. Courses are intended for authors, game designers, and hobbyists. A free course is available to get you started! See the website or mailing list for details: http://www.worldbuilding.university/.

THE PODCAST

The Art of World Building podcast expands on the material within the series. The additional examples offer world builders more insight into ramifications of decisions. You can hear the podcast, read transcripts, and learn more about the episodes: Visit http://www.artofworldbuilding.com/podcasts.

YOUTUBE CHANNEL

The Art of World Building YouTube channel now has videos that also expand on the material within the series. Check out the growing playlists and subscribe. Videos include replays of webinars that feature a Q&A, lessons from the books, previews of WBU courses, and tips from the book, *185 Tips on World Building*. Visit http://bit.ly/AOWBYouTube.

THE UNIVERSE

In this section, you will decide on galaxies, solar systems, and other elements in space.

THE GALAXY

What is the name of the galaxy where the story takes place? What kind is it (such as spiral)?

_____

What are the names of the nearest galaxies?

_____

Draw the locations of the galaxies in relation to each other.

Draw the galaxy and indicate the position of each solar system you need.

THE SOLAR SYSTEM

What is the name of the solar system?

_____

What type of star does it have (yellow, red dwarf) and does it have a name? Are there two stars? How old is it?

_____

How many planets are there?

_____

Are there any named comets or asteroids? How often do they orbit?

_____

Is there an asteroid field? Where is it?

_____

Are there any destroyed planets?

_____

NOTEWORTHY LOCATIONS

Are there any man-made objects like space stations, satellites, or bases? Indicate if they are tidally locked to what they orbit so that one side always faces it.

Location Name	**Location Name**	**Location Name**
Type	Type	Type

Is it tidally locked?   Yes   No
Orbit (circle one):
     Circular   Elliptical
     Retrograde? Yes No
What does it orbit?
	Is it tidally locked? Yes No
	Orbit (circle one):
	     Circular Elliptical
	     Retrograde? Yes No
	What does it orbit?
		Is it tidally locked? Yes No
		Orbit (circle one):
		     Circular Elliptical
		     Retrograde? Yes No
		What does it orbit?

Age:	Age:	Age:
Condition:	Condition:	Condition:
Purpose:	Purpose:	Purpose:
Population:	Population:	Population:
Noteworthy features:	Noteworthy features:	Noteworthy features:

Location Name	Location Name	Location Name
Type	Type	Type

Is it tidally locked? Yes No
Orbit (circle one):
   Circular   Elliptical
   Retrograde? Yes No
What does it orbit?
	Is it tidally locked? Yes No
	Orbit (circle one):
	   Circular Elliptical
	   Retrograde? Yes No
	What does it orbit?
		Is it tidally locked? Yes No
		Orbit (circle one):
		   Circular Elliptical
		   Retrograde? Yes No
		What does it orbit?

Age:	Age:	Age:
Condition:	Condition:	Condition:
Purpose:	Purpose:	Purpose:
Population:	Population:	Population:
Noteworthy features:	Noteworthy features:	Noteworthy features:

THE PLANET

In this section, you will create the planet described in this workbook.

What is the planet's name and nickname?

_____

What type of planet is it (rocky, ice, or gas)? Does it have an atmosphere and is it breathable? by humans or another species? How far from the star is it? Is it in the habitable zone? What is the temperature range?

_____

_____

_____

What is the axial tilt (23.5 degrees like Earth)? Does it orbit counterclockwise or clockwise? Is it tidally locked to the sun? How long does it take, in days, to orbit the sun?

_____

_____

_____

Does the planet have a ring system?. If yes, what is it made of? Ice, gas, stone?

_____

Planet orbit direction: Clockwise   Counterclockwise

Is there ever a conjunction of heavenly bodies? Which ones are included and how often does it occur?

_____

_____

Draw the planet and its moons, rings, or prominent space stations.

UNIVERSAL TIME

Some elements of time will remain constant across a world (such as days in a year) , while others will vary by the sovereign power, but you need a universal calendar to correlate events across kingdoms with varying time measurements. Decide these universal measurements here.

How many days are in a year? Does it ever change and how often?

_____

_____

How many days are in a week?

_____

How many weeks are in a month? Or does it vary?

_____

How many months are in a year?

_____

How many hours are in a day?

_____

How many minutes are in an hour?

_____

How many seconds are in a minute?

_____

Are hours measured sequentially like military time or divided in another way, like AM and PM?

_____

_____

_____

How many seasons exist and what are they?

_____

_____

_____

_____

From what sovereign power did the universal calendar originate?

_____

What abbreviation is used to indicate the years, such as B.C. or A.D. on Earth? What does it mean?

_____

_____

_____

_____

_____

MONTHS

List the months in order, leaving blank ones that aren't needed. Symbols can be zodiacs, associated gods, etc.

Month 1	Month 2	Month 3
Name	Name	Name
Season	Season	Season
Earth equivalent	Earth equivalent	Earth equivalent
Symbol(s)	Symbol(s)	Symbol(s)
Stone	Stone	Stone
Flower:	Flower:	Flower:
Other	Other	Other
Special Events;;	Special Events;;	Special Events;;

Month 4	Month 5	Month 6
Name	Name	Name
Season	Season	Season
Earth equivalent	Earth equivalent	Earth equivalent
Symbol(s)	Symbol(s)	Symbol(s)
Stone	Stone	Stone
Flower:	Flower:	Flower:
Other	Other	Other
Special Events;;	Special Events;;	Special Events;;

Month 7	Month 8	Month 9
Name	Name	Name
Season	Season	Season
Earth equivalent	Earth equivalent	Earth equivalent
Symbol(s)	Symbol(s)	Symbol(s)
Stone	Stone	Stone
Flower:	Flower:	Flower:
Other	Other	Other
Special Events;;	Special Events;;	Special Events;;

Month 10	Month 11	Month 12
Name	Name	Name
Season	Season	Season
Earth equivalent	Earth equivalent	Earth equivalent
Symbol(s)	Symbol(s)	Symbol(s)
Stone	Stone	Stone
Flower:	Flower:	Flower:
Other	Other	Other
Special Events;;	Special Events;;	Special Events;;

Month 13	Month 14	Month 15
Name	Name	Name
Season	Season	Season
Earth equivalent	Earth equivalent	Earth equivalent
Symbol(s)	Symbol(s)	Symbol(s)
Stone	Stone	Stone
Flower:	Flower:	Flower:
Other	Other	Other
Special Events;;	Special Events;;	Special Events;;

MOONS

For high-level information on moon, fill out this chart. For moon position, use "1" to indicate which is closest, etc.

Moon Name	Moon Name	Moon Name
Position	Position	Position

Is it tidally locked?   Yes   No
Orbit (circle one):
    Circular   Elliptical
    Retrograde? Yes No
Is it habitable? Yes No
	Is it tidally locked? Yes No
	Orbit (circle one):
	    Circular Elliptical
	    Retrograde? Yes No
	Is it habitable? Yes No
		Is it tidally locked? Yes No
		Orbit (circle one):
		    Circular Elliptical
		    Retrograde? Yes No
		Is it habitable? Yes No

Moon Name	Moon Name	Moon Name
Position	Position	Position

Is it tidally locked?   Yes   No
Orbit (circle one):
    Circular   Elliptical
    Retrograde? Yes No
Is it habitable? Yes No
	Is it tidally locked? Yes No
	Orbit (circle one):
	    Circular Elliptical
	    Retrograde? Yes No
	Is it habitable? Yes No
		Is it tidally locked? Yes No
		Orbit (circle one):
		    Circular Elliptical
		    Retrograde? Yes No
		Is it habitable? Yes No

If more detail is required for a moon, enter it below.

_____

_____

_____

_____

_____

_____

_____

CONSTELLATIONS

What constellations exist?

Constellation Name	**Constellation Name**	**Constellation Name**
_____	_____	_____
Hemisphere? Northern Southern	Hemisphere? Northern Southern	Hemisphere? Northern Southern
Symbol:	Symbol:	Symbol:
_____	_____	_____
_____	_____	_____
Is it a dark constellation? Yes No	Is it a dark constellation? Yes No	Is it a dark constellation? Yes No
Important stars within:	Important stars within:	Important stars within:
_____	_____	_____
_____	_____	_____
_____	_____	_____
Draw it:	Draw it:	Draw it:

NOTES

Write down additional considerations for this planet

_____

_____

_____

_____

_____

_____

_____

_____

_____

_____

_____

_____

_____

_____

_____

_____

_____

_____

LAND AND SEA

In this section, you will create the continents and major water bodies.

CONTINENTS

Draw the continents in relation to each other. Don't worry about their shape and contour of each much. If desired, use a ruler and pencil to draw a horizonal line for the equator.

At a high level, decide how many continents this planet has and their features. Also decide which ones are considered east or west on world maps

Continent Name	Continent Name	Continent Name
Hemisphere? Southern Northern Location	Hemisphere? Southern Northern Location	Hemisphere? Southern Northern Location
Percent above/below equator	Percent above/below equator	Percent above/below equator
Notable sovereign powers and type	Notable sovereign powers and type	Notable sovereign powers and type
Notable cities and location/power	Notable cities and location/power	Notable cities and location/power
Other	Other	Other

Continent Name	Continent Name	Continent Name
Hemisphere? Southern Northern Location	Hemisphere? Southern Northern Location	Hemisphere? Southern Northern Location
Percent above/below equator	Percent above/below equator	Percent above/below equator
Notable sovereign powers and type	Notable sovereign powers and type	Notable sovereign powers and type
Notable cities and location/power	Notable cities and location/power	Notable cities and location/power
Other	Other	Other

Continent Name	Continent Name	Continent Name
Hemisphere? Southern Northern Location	Hemisphere? Southern Northern Location	Hemisphere? Southern Northern Location
Percent above/below equator	Percent above/below equator	Percent above/below equator
Notable sovereign powers and type	Notable sovereign powers and type	Notable sovereign powers and type
Notable cities and location/power	Notable cities and location/power	Notable cities and location/power
Other	Other	Other

NOTES ON CONTINENTS

_____

_____

_____

_____

_____

_____

_____

_____

_____

_____

_____

_____

_____

_____

_____

_____

_____

_____

_____

_____

ISLANDS

Are there any large islands of note? Indicate their names and which continent, if any, they are near, and what body of water is their home. Indicate how large and noteworthy elements, including population makeup.

Island Name	Island Name	Island Name
Hemisphere? Southern Northern	Hemisphere? Southern Northern	Hemisphere? Southern Northern
Nearest continent and direction	Nearest continent and direction	Nearest continent and direction
Noteworthy features or settlements	Noteworthy features or settlements	Noteworthy features or settlements
Island Name	Island Name	Island Name
Hemisphere? Southern Northern	Hemisphere? Southern Northern	Hemisphere? Southern Northern
Nearest continent and direction	Nearest continent and direction	Nearest continent and direction
Noteworthy features or settlements	Noteworthy features or settlements	Noteworthy features or settlements

Island Name	Island Name	Island Name
Hemisphere? Southern Northern	Hemisphere? Southern Northern	Hemisphere? Southern Northern
Nearest continent and direction	Nearest continent and direction	Nearest continent and direction
Noteworthy features or settlements	Noteworthy features or settlements	Noteworthy features or settlements

OCEANS AND SEAS

Name the oceans and seas, indicating their position (you can use the previous map, too).

_____

_____

_____

_____

_____

_____

_____

_____

What is the continent's name and does it mean anything?

_____

_____

Draw the continent and indicate oceans, large water bodies, major rivers, and islands. Include major mountain ranges, forests, grasslands, and deserts. You can optionally indicate sovereign powers, but focus on land features first.

Which hemisphere is it found on, or does it span the equator?

_____

MOUNTAINS

Indicate high level details on the mountain ranges

Mountain Range Name/Nickname	Mountain Range Name/Nickname	Mountain Range Name/Nickname
Direction	Direction	Direction
Average height	Average height	Average height
Location: Coastal Interior	Location: Coastal Interior	Location: Coastal Interior
Region/Powers spanned	Region/Powers spanned	Region/Powers spanned
Species/animals here	Species/animals here	Species/animals here
Important elements	Important elements	Important elements

Mountain Range Name/Nickname	**Mountain Range Name/Nickname**	**Mountain Range Name/Nickname**
Direction	Direction	Direction
Average height	Average height	Average height
Location: Coastal Interior	Location: Coastal Interior	Location: Coastal Interior
Region/Powers spanned	Region/Powers spanned	Region/Powers spanned
Species/animals here	Species/animals here	Species/animals here
Important elements	Important elements	Important elements

FORESTS

Indicate high level details on the major forests found on the continent.

Forest Name/Nickname	Forest Name/Nickname	Forest Name/Nickname
_____	_____	_____
Type: Forest Woodland Savannah Jungle	Type: Forest Woodland Savannah Jungle	Type: Forest Woodland Savannah Jungle
Region/Powers spanned	Region/Powers spanned	Region/Powers spanned
Species/animals here	Species/animals here	Species/animals here
Is it passable? Easily? Roads exist?	Is it passable? Easily? Roads exist?	Is it passable? Easily? Roads exist?
Important elements	Important elements	Important elements

Forest Name/Nickname

_____

Type: Forest Woodland
       Savannah Jungle

Region/Powers spanned

_____

_____

_____

Species/animals here

_____

_____

_____

_____

Is it passable? Easily? Roads exist?

_____

_____

Important elements

_____

_____

_____

_____

_____

Forest Name/Nickname

_____

Type: Forest Woodland
       Savannah Jungle

Region/Powers spanned

_____

_____

_____

Species/animals here

_____

_____

_____

_____

Is it passable? Easily? Roads exist?

_____

_____

Important elements

_____

_____

_____

_____

_____

Forest Name/Nickname

_____

Type: Forest Woodland
       Savannah Jungle

Region/Powers spanned

_____

_____

_____

Species/animals here

_____

_____

_____

_____

Is it passable? Easily? Roads exist?

_____

_____

Important elements

_____

_____

_____

_____

_____

DESERTS

Indicate high level details on the major deserts found on the continent.

Desert Name/Nickname	Desert Name/Nickname	Desert Name/Nickname
Type: Hot Cold Ground: Sand Hard Earth Altitude	Type: Hot Cold Ground: Sand Hard Earth Altitude	Type: Hot Cold Ground: Sand Hard Earth Altitude
Region/Powers spanned	Region/Powers spanned	Region/Powers spanned
Species/animals here	Species/animals here	Species/animals here
Important elements	Important elements	Important elements

Desert Name/Nickname	Desert Name/Nickname	Desert Name/Nickname

Type: Hot   Cold
Ground: Sand   Hard Earth

Altitude

Region/Powers spanned

Species/animals here

Important elements

Type: Hot   Cold
Ground: Sand   Hard Earth

Altitude

Region/Powers spanned

Species/animals here

Important elements

Type: Hot   Cold
Ground: Sand   Hard Earth

Altitude

Region/Powers spanned

Species/animals here

Important elements

WATERWAYS AND WETLANDS

Indicate high level details on the major desert found on the continent. Depth will determine the speed of a river.

Name/Nickname	Name/Nickname	Name/Nickname
Type: River Lake Depth: Shallow Deep	Type: River Lake Depth: Shallow Deep	Type: River Lake Depth: Shallow Deep
Mountain source(s)	Mountain source(s)	Mountain source(s)
Region/Powers spanned	Region/Powers spanned	Region/Powers spanned
Wetland: Bog Fen Marsh Swamp Wetland location: N E S W	Wetland: Bog Fen Marsh Swamp Wetland location: N E S W	Wetland: Bog Fen Marsh Swamp Wetland location: N E S W
Species/animals in water or wetland	Species/animals in water or wetland	Species/animals in water or wetland

Name/Nickname	Name/Nickname	Name/Nickname
_____	_____	_____
Type: River Lake Depth: Shallow Deep	Type: River Lake Depth: Shallow Deep	Type: River Lake Depth: Shallow Deep
Mountain source(s)	Mountain source(s)	Mountain source(s)
_____ _____	_____ _____	_____ _____
Region/Powers spanned	Region/Powers spanned	Region/Powers spanned
_____ _____	_____ _____	_____ _____
Wetland: Bog Fen Marsh Swamp Wetland location: N E S W	Wetland: Bog Fen Marsh Swamp Wetland location: N E S W	Wetland: Bog Fen Marsh Swamp Wetland location: N E S W
_____ _____	_____ _____	_____ _____
Species/animals in water or wetland	Species/animals in water or wetland	Species/animals in water or wetland
_____ _____ _____ _____ _____ _____	_____ _____ _____ _____ _____ _____	_____ _____ _____ _____ _____ _____

Name/Nickname	Name/Nickname	Name/Nickname
Type: River Lake	Type: River Lake	Type: River Lake
Depth: Shallow Deep	Depth: Shallow Deep	Depth: Shallow Deep
Mountain source(s)	Mountain source(s)	Mountain source(s)
Region/Powers spanned	Region/Powers spanned	Region/Powers spanned
Wetland: Bog Fen Marsh Swamp	Wetland: Bog Fen Marsh Swamp	Wetland: Bog Fen Marsh Swamp
Wetland location: N E S W	Wetland location: N E S W	Wetland location: N E S W
Species/animals in water or wetland	Species/animals in water or wetland	Species/animals in water or wetland

PLANTS

Plant Name/Nickname	Plant Name/Nickname	Plant Name/Nickname
Earth equivalent(s)	Earth equivalent(s)	Earth equivalent(s)
Climate:	Climate:	Climate:
Season planted:	Season planted:	Season planted:
Harvested:	Harvested:	Harvested:
Texture:	Texture:	Texture:
Toxicity:	Toxicity:	Toxicity:
Appearance:	Appearance:	Appearance:
Smell, taste:	Smell, taste:	Smell, taste:
Products/uses:	Products/uses:	Products/uses:

Plant Name/Nickname	Plant Name/Nickname	Plant Name/Nickname
Earth equivalent(s)	Earth equivalent(s)	Earth equivalent(s)
Climate:	Climate:	Climate:
Season planted:	Season planted:	Season planted:
Harvested:	Harvested:	Harvested:
Texture:	Texture:	Texture:
Toxicity:	Toxicity:	Toxicity:
Appearance:	Appearance:	Appearance:
Smell, taste:	Smell, taste:	Smell, taste:
Products/uses:	Products/uses:	Products/uses:

NOTES ABOUT THE PLANTS

ANIMALS

Animal Name/Nickname	Animal Name/Nickname	Animal Name/Nickname
Type (mammal, fish, bird, etc.):	Type (mammal, fish, bird, etc.):	Type (mammal, fish, bird, etc.):
Earth equivalent(s)	Earth equivalent(s)	Earth equivalent(s)
Lifespan	Lifespan	Lifespan
Mating season, litter size, litter type (eggs, live birth):	Mating season, litter size, litter type (eggs, live birth):	Mating season, litter size, litter type (eggs, live birth):
Habitat/climate:	Habitat/climate:	Habitat/climate:
Solitary or pack	Solitary or pack	Solitary or pack
Prey: Herbivore Carnivore Omnivore	**Prey:** Herbivore Carnivore Omnivore	**Prey:** Herbivore Carnivore Omnivore
Predators:	Predators:	Predators:

Animal Name/Nickname	Animal Name/Nickname	Animal Name/Nickname
Type (mammal, fish, bird, etc.):	Type (mammal, fish, bird, etc.):	Type (mammal, fish, bird, etc.):
Earth equivalent(s)	Earth equivalent(s)	Earth equivalent(s)
Lifespan	Lifespan	Lifespan
Mating season, litter size, litter type (eggs, live birth):	Mating season, litter size, litter type (eggs, live birth):	Mating season, litter size, litter type (eggs, live birth):
Habitat/climate:	Habitat/climate:	Habitat/climate:
Solitary or pack	Solitary or pack	Solitary or pack
Prey: Herbivore Carnivore Omnivore	**Prey:** Herbivore Carnivore Omnivore	**Prey:** Herbivore Carnivore Omnivore
Predators:	Predators:	Predators:

NOTES ABOUT THE ANIMALS

Sovereign Powers

In this section, you will decide on several sovereign powers in detail. Virtually all stories take place in one, with others nearby impacting outlook, from products to safety, travel, and visitors. But not all need in depth development. The main power does, while some details can be skimped on others.

Sovereign Power 1

What is the name of this power?

_____

What is the current type of government?

_____

What are the three most recent types of government? Indicate their legacy.

Type 1	Type 2	Type 3
_____	_____	_____
Year Founded:	Year Founded:	Year Founded:
Year Destroyed and cause:	Year Destroyed and cause:	Year Destroyed and cause:
Notes	Notes	Notes

LEADERSHIP

What is the name and title of the head of state? List gender, age, and race.

_____

_____

If a different person, what is the name and title of the head of government? List gender, age, and race.

_____

_____

Is there a group or organization that influences leadership? What is their name? Describe their goals, tactics, reputation.

_____

_____

_____

_____

_____

IDENTIFIERS

What is this power famous for?

_____

_____

What are the symbols, banners, slogans, and colors?

_____

_____

_____

_____

_____

HISTORY

Define three events that are impacting life today. Focus on what is useable in your storyline or character development.

_____

_____

_____

_____

_____

_____

_____

_____

_____

_____

_____

_____

_____

_____

_____

_____

_____

_____

LOCATION

On what continent is this power located?

_____

Draw a rough shape of this continent and indicate where this sovereign power is found, drawing its outline.

Which powers are adjacent to this one? Indicate their name and direction from here.

_____

_____

_____

_____

What sorts of terrain exist here? Circle each.

Grasslands   Desserts   Mountains

Forests Types: **Wetlands Types**   Hills
Forest Woodland Savannah Jungle   Fens Bogs Marshes Swamps

What climates exist and in what regions?

_____

_____

_____

_____

What unique or noteworthy places has this power built or controlled?

_____

_____

_____

What are the important settlements in this power? They can be further defined in the settlements section.

Settlement Name	Settlement Name	Settlement Name
_____	_____	_____
Type City Town Village Other	Type City Town Village Other	Type City Town Village Other
Size: Large Moderate Small	Size: Large Moderate Small	Size: Large Moderate Small
Year Founded; _____	Year Founded; _____	Year Founded; _____
Symbol: _____	Symbol: _____	Symbol: _____
Colors: _____	Colors: _____	Colors: _____
Location:	Location:	Location:
_____	_____	_____
Terrain: Mountain Hills Forest Desert Plains	Terrain: Mountain Hills Forest Desert Plains	Terrain: Mountain Hills Forest Desert Plains
Species/races present	Species/races present	Species/races present
_____	_____	_____
_____	_____	_____
_____	_____	_____
_____	_____	_____

Settlement Name

Type City Town Village Other

Size: Large Moderate Small

Year Founded;

Symbol:

Colors:

Location:

Terrain: Mountain Hills Forest
        Desert   Plains

Species/races present

Settlement Name

Type City Town Village Other

Size: Large Moderate Small

Year Founded;

Symbol:

Colors:

Location:

Terrain: Mountain Hills Forest
        Desert   Plains

Species/races present

Settlement Name

Type City Town Village Other

Size: Large Moderate Small

Year Founded;

Symbol:

Colors:

Location:

Terrain: Mountain Hills Forest
        Desert   Plains

Species/races present

NOTES ON THESE SETTLEMENTS

Settlement Name	Settlement Name	Settlement Name
Type City Town Village Other	Type City Town Village Other	Type City Town Village Other
Size: Large Moderate Small	Size: Large Moderate Small	Size: Large Moderate Small
Year Founded;	Year Founded;	Year Founded;
Symbol:	Symbol:	Symbol:
Colors:	Colors:	Colors:
Location:	Location:	Location:
Terrain: Mountain Hills Forest Desert Plains	Terrain: Mountain Hills Forest Desert Plains	Terrain: Mountain Hills Forest Desert Plains
Species/races present	Species/races present	Species/races present

NOTES ON THESE SETTLEMENTS

SOVEREIGN POWER MAP

Draw this power and indicate major features like settlements, forests, etc.

WORLD VIEW

What languages are spoken in this power? Which ones are forbidden?

_____

_____

_____

_____

_____

What customs originated or are associated with this power?

_____

_____

_____

_____

_____

_____

_____

What is the work week like? How many days per week, hours per day, are people expected to work? Is there a siesta? Do people live comfortable or hard lives? What are their prospects for retirement?

_____

_____

_____

_____

_____

What monetary system is generally accepted here? The details should be in the later workbook section for this.

_____

_____

What education systems exist in this settlement?

_____

_____

_____

_____

_____

What kind of legal system do they have? Is this a civil, common, or religious legal system? If the latter, what god?

_____

_____

Create laws, which can originate from morality or past incidents.

_____

_____

_____

_____

———————————————————————

———————————————————————

———————————————————————

———————————————————————

———————————————————————

———————————————————————

———————————————————————

What crimes and punishments exist? These are defined in another section.

———————————————————————

———————————————————————

———————————————————————

———————————————————————

———————————————————————

———————————————————————

———————————————————————

———————————————————————

RELATIONSHIPS

What is this power's relationship with other powers? Some may be allies, other enemies.

———————————————————————

———————————————————————

_____

_____

_____

_____

_____

Are there organizations that exist within this power, perhaps despite attempts to eradicate them?

_____

_____

_____

_____

What armed forces does this power have?

_____

_____

_____

_____

Are there any characters who are noteworthy throughout the power? For what? What is their status and location?

_____

_____

_____

_____

What species/races are here, in what percentages, and where do they congregate? Who is welcomed and shunned?

Species/Race Name	Species/Race Name	Species/Race Name
How common are they?	How common are they?	How common are they?
Where are most of them?	Where are most of them?	Where are most of them?
How are they viewed?	How are they viewed?	How are they viewed?

Species/Race Name	Species/Race Name	Species/Race Name
How common are they?	How common are they?	How common are they?
Where are most of them?	Where are most of them?	Where are most of them?
How are they viewed?	How are they viewed?	How are they viewed?

Species/Race Name	Species/Race Name	Species/Race Name
How common are they?	How common are they?	How common are they?
Where are most of them?	Where are most of them?	Where are most of them?
How are they viewed?	How are they viewed?	How are they viewed?

FINAL NOTES

_____

_____

_____

_____

_____

_____

_____

_____

SOVEREIGN POWER 2

What is the name of this power?

_____

What is the current type of government?

_____

What are the three most recent types of government? Indicate their legacy.

Type 1	Type 2	Type 3
_____	_____	_____
Year Founded:	Year Founded:	Year Founded:
Year Destroyed and cause:	Year Destroyed and cause:	Year Destroyed and cause:
Notes	Notes	Notes

LEADERSHIP

What is the name and title of the head of state? List gender, age, and race.

_____

_____

_____

_____

If a different person, what is the name and title of the head of government? List gender, age, and race.

_____

_____

_____

Is there a group or organization that influences leadership? What is their name? Describe their goals, tactics, reputation.

_____

_____

_____

_____

_____

IDENTIFIERS

What is this power famous for?

_____

_____

What are the symbols, banners, slogans, and colors?

_____

_____

_____

_____

_____

_____

_____

_____

_____

HISTORY

Define three events that are impacting life today. Focus on what is useable in your storyline or character development.

_____

_____

_____

_____

_____

_____

_____

_____

_____

_____

_____

_____

_____

_____

_____

_____

_____

_____

_____

_____

LOCATION

On what continent is this power located?

Draw a rough shape of this continent and indicate where this sovereign power is found, drawing its outline.

Which powers are adjacent to this one? Indicate their name and direction from here.

What sorts of terrain exist here? Circle each.

Grasslands

Desserts

Mountains

Forests Types:
Forest Woodland Savannah Jungle

Wetlands Types
Fens Bogs Marshes Swamps

Hills

What climates exist and in what regions?

_____

_____

What unique or noteworthy places has this power built or controlled?

_____

_____

_____

_____

What are the important settlements in this power? They can be further defined in the settlements section.

Settlement Name	**Settlement Name**	**Settlement Name**
Type City Town Village Other	Type City Town Village Other	Type City Town Village Other
Size: Large Moderate Small	Size: Large Moderate Small	Size: Large Moderate Small
Year Founded;	Year Founded;	Year Founded;
Symbol:	Symbol:	Symbol:
Colors:	Colors:	Colors:
Location:	Location:	Location:
Terrain: Mountain Hills Forest Desert Plains	Terrain: Mountain Hills Forest Desert Plains	Terrain: Mountain Hills Forest Desert Plains
Species/races present	Species/races present	Species/races present

Settlement Name	Settlement Name	Settlement Name
Type City Town Village Other	Type City Town Village Other	Type City Town Village Other
Size: Large Moderate Small	Size: Large Moderate Small	Size: Large Moderate Small
Year Founded;	Year Founded;	Year Founded;
Symbol:	Symbol:	Symbol:
Colors:	Colors:	Colors:
Location:	Location:	Location:
Terrain: Mountain Hills Forest Desert Plains	Terrain: Mountain Hills Forest Desert Plains	Terrain: Mountain Hills Forest Desert Plains
Species/races present	Species/races present	Species/races present

NOTES ON THESE SETTLEMENTS

_____

_____

_____

_____

_____

_____

Settlement Name

Type City Town Village Other

Size: Large Moderate Small

Year Founded;

Symbol:

Colors:

Location:

Terrain: Mountain Hills Forest
          Desert Plains

Species/races present

Settlement Name

Type City Town Village Other

Size: Large Moderate Small

Year Founded;

Symbol:

Colors:

Location:

Terrain: Mountain Hills Forest
          Desert Plains

Species/races present

Settlement Name

Type City Town Village Other

Size: Large Moderate Small

Year Founded;

Symbol:

Colors:

Location:

Terrain: Mountain Hills Forest
          Desert Plains

Species/races present

NOTES ON THESE SETTLEMENTS

SOVEREIGN POWER MAP

Draw this power and indicate major features like settlements, forests, etc.

WORLD VIEW

What languages are spoken in this power? Which ones are forbidden?

_____

_____

_____

_____

_____

_____

What customs originated or are associated with this power?

_____

_____

_____

_____

_____

_____

_____

_____

_____

What is the work week like? How many days per week, hours per day, are people expected to work? Is there a siesta? Do people live comfortable or hard lives? What are their prospects for retirement?

_____

_____

_____

_____

_____

_____

_____

What monetary system is generally accepted here? The details should be in the later workbook section for this.

_____

_____

What education systems exist in this settlement?

_____

_____

_____

_____

_____

What kind of legal system do they have? Is this a civil, common, or religious legal system? If the latter, what god?

_____

_____

_____

Create laws, which can originate from morality or past incidents.

_____

_____

_____

_____

_____

_____

_____

_____

_____

_____

_____

_____

What crimes and punishments exist? These are defined in another section.

_____

_____

_____

_____

_____

_____

_____

_____

RELATIONSHIPS

What is this power's relationship with other powers? Some may be allies, other enemies.

_____

_____

_____

_____

_____

_____

_____

_____

Are there organizations that exist within this power, perhaps despite attempts to eradicate them?

_____

_____

_____

_____

What armed forces does this power have?

_____

_____

_____

_____

Are there any characters who are noteworthy throughout the power? For what? What is their status and location?

_____

_____

_____

What species/races are here, in what percentages, and where do they congregate? Who is welcomed and shunned?

Species/Race Name	**Species/Race Name**	**Species/Race Name**
How common are they?	How common are they?	How common are they?
Where are most of them?	Where are most of them?	Where are most of them?
How are they viewed?	How are they viewed?	How are they viewed?
Species/Race Name	**Species/Race Name**	**Species/Race Name**
How common are they?	How common are they?	How common are they?
Where are most of them?	Where are most of them?	Where are most of them?
How are they viewed?	How are they viewed?	How are they viewed?

Species/Race Name	Species/Race Name	Species/Race Name
How common are they?	How common are they?	How common are they?
Where are most of them?	Where are most of them?	Where are most of them?
How are they viewed?	How are they viewed?	How are they viewed?

FINAL NOTES

SETTLEMENTS

In this section, you will create multiple settlements in more detail than what you listed in the sovereign powers section. These should be the ones you intend to use most rather than in passing.

SETTLEMENT 1

What is the settlement name? Is there a nickname?

_____

Is this a city, town, village, castle, outpost, or something else?

_____

If this settlement is famous for everything, list it here.

_____

_____

_____

_____

_____

IDENTIFIERS

What is the symbol, banner, or flag? What does it signify?

_____

_____

What are the settlement colors? What do they signify?

Is there a slogan associated with it?

LOCATION

If it is part of a sovereign power, indicate which one. Has it been part of others before and changed hands?

What is the climate and terrain (forests, mountainous, desert, plain, sea/river port?)? The latter is not only what is inside the settlement but what surrounds it and in what directions?

SETTLEMENT MAP

Draw this settlement and its immediate surroundings.

What other settlements are nearby? Indicate them on the map or state the direction and distance from here.

_____

_____

_____

_____

_____

Are there any important or distinctive features here?

_____

_____

_____

_____

_____

What sort of fortifications exist and in what condition are they?

_____

_____

_____

_____

_____

What kind of armed forces exist here? Is the settlement known for it? Do training centers exist?

_____

_____

_____

_____

What products are created here? Use the local land features for inspiration. What products do they want from elsewhere?

_____

_____

_____

_____

HISTORY

Year founded: _____

What significant wars or battles have taken place here?

_____

_____

_____

_____

Are there any memorable events in the settlement's past? How did they shape the present?

_____

_____

_____

THE INHABITANTS

Who is the current leader and what is their title? How long have they been in power?

_____

_____

_____

Are there any individuals or organization, either based here or not, that influence events? What do they want?

_____

_____

_____

_____

_____

_____

Are there any important individuals living here now, in the past, or who grew up here?

_____

_____

_____

_____

Are there any monsters or creatures in or around the settlement? Describe location and past incidents.

_____

_____

_____

_____

_____

_____

_____

_____

_____

_____

_____

What species and races are here? How common are they, how are they treated/viewed/welcomed?

Species/Race Name	Species/Race Name	Species/Race Name
_____	_____	_____
How common are they?	How common are they?	How common are they?
_____	_____	_____
_____	_____	_____
How are they viewed?	How are they viewed?	How are they viewed?
_____	_____	_____
_____	_____	_____
_____	_____	_____

Species/Race Name	Species/Race Name	Species/Race Name
_____	_____	_____
How common are they?	How common are they?	How common are they?
_____	_____	_____
_____	_____	_____
How are they viewed?	How are they viewed?	How are they viewed?
_____	_____	_____
_____	_____	_____
_____	_____	_____

OTHER DETAILS

What religions are practiced here? Which ones are shunned?

_____

_____

_____

_____

_____

What monetary system is used? Does it differ from the sovereign power this might be part of?

_____

_____

What local laws exist about the use of magic or technology?

_____

_____

_____

_____

_____

_____

_____

What other laws, crimes, and punishment exist here? You may have defined them in another section.

_____

_____

_____

_____

_____

_____

Are there any phenomena here? What impact do they have? Where are they located?

_____

_____

_____

_____

_____

_____

Are there any important locations in town, such as important buildings beyond what is usually expected (like city hall)?

_____

_____

_____

_____

What festivals and holidays are unique to this location?

_____

_____

_____

_____

What education systems exist here? You may have defined them in another section.

_____

_____

_____

_____

_____

FINAL NOTES

SETTLEMENT 2

What is the settlement name? Is there a nickname?

_____

Is this a city, town, village, castle, outpost, or something else?

_____

If this settlement is famous for everything, list it here.

_____

_____

_____

_____

_____

_____

IDENTIFIERS

What is the symbol, banner, or flag? What does it signify?

_____

_____

_____

What are the settlement colors? What do they signify?

_____

_____

Is there a slogan associated with it?

_____

_____

LOCATION

If it is part of a sovereign power, indicate which one. Has it been part of others before and changed hands?

_____

_____

_____

_____

_____

_____

What is the climate and terrain (forests, mountainous, desert, plain, sea/river port?)? The latter is not only what is inside the settlement but what surrounds it and in what directions?

_____

_____

_____

_____

_____

_____

_____

_____

_____

_____

_____

SETTLEMENT MAP

Draw this settlement and its immediate surroundings.

What other settlements are nearby? Indicate them on the map or state the direction and distance from here.

_____

_____

_____

_____

_____

Are there any important or distinctive features here?

_____

_____

_____

_____

_____

What sort of fortifications exist and in what condition are they?

_____

_____

_____

_____

_____

What kind of armed forces exist here? Is the settlement known for it? Do training centers exist?

_____

_____

_____

_____

_____

What products are created here? Use the local land features for inspiration. What products do they want from elsewhere?

_____

_____

_____

_____

HISTORY

Year founded: _____

What significant wars or battles have taken place here?

_____

_____

_____

_____

Are there any memorable events in the settlement's past? How did they shape the present?

_____

_____

_____

_____

THE INHABITANTS

Who is the current leader and what is their title? How long have they been in power?

_____

_____

_____

_____

Are there any individuals or organization, either based here or not, that influence events? What do they want?

_____

_____

_____

_____

_____

_____

_____

Are there any important individuals living here now, in the past, or who grew up here?

_____

_____

_____

Are there any monsters or creatures in or around the settlement? Describe location and past incidents.

_____

_____

_____

_____

_____

_____

_____

_____

_____

_____

What species and races are here? How common are they, how are they treated/viewed/welcomed?

Species/Race Name	Species/Race Name	Species/Race Name
How common are they?	How common are they?	How common are they?
How are they viewed?	How are they viewed?	How are they viewed?

Species/Race Name	Species/Race Name	Species/Race Name
How common are they?	How common are they?	How common are they?
How are they viewed?	How are they viewed?	How are they viewed?

OTHER DETAILS

What religions are practiced here? Which ones are shunned?

_____

_____

_____

_____

What monetary system is used? Does it differ from the sovereign power this might be part of?

_____

_____

What local laws exist about the use of magic or technology?

_____

_____

_____

_____

_____

_____

_____

What other laws, crimes, and punishment exist here? You may have defined them in another section.

_____

_____

_____

_____

_____

_____

Are there any phenomena here? What impact do they have? Where are they located?

_____

_____

_____

_____

_____

Are there any important locations in town, such as important buildings beyond what is usually expected (like city hall)?

_____

_____

_____

_____

What festivals and holidays are unique to this location?

_____

_____

_____

_____

What education systems exist here? You may have defined them in another section.

_____

_____

_____

_____

_____

FINAL NOTES

_____

_____

_____

_____

_____

_____

_____

_____

_____

_____

_____

_____

_____

_____

_____

_____

_____

_____

_____

_____

Settlement 3

What is the settlement name? Is there a nickname?

Is this a city, town, village, castle, outpost, or something else?

If this settlement is famous for everything, list it here.

Identifiers

What is the symbol, banner, or flag? What does it signify?

What are the settlement colors? What do they signify?

Is there a slogan associated with it?

LOCATION

If it is part of a sovereign power, indicate which one. Has it been part of others before and changed hands?

_____

_____

_____

_____

_____

What is the climate and terrain (forests, mountainous, desert, plain, sea/river port?)? The latter is not only what is inside the settlement but what surrounds it and in what directions?

_____

_____

_____

_____

_____

_____

_____

_____

_____

_____

_____

Settlement Map

Draw this settlement and its immediate surroundings.

What other settlements are nearby? Indicate them on the map or state the direction and distance from here.

_____

_____

_____

_____

_____

Are there any important or distinctive features here?

_____

_____

_____

_____

_____

What sort of fortifications exist and in what condition are they?

_____

_____

_____

_____

_____

What kind of armed forces exist here? Is the settlement known for it? Do training centers exist?

_____

_____

_____

_____

_____

What products are created here? Use the local land features for inspiration. What products do they want from elsewhere?

_____

_____

_____

_____

HISTORY

Year founded: _____

What significant wars or battles have taken place here?

_____

_____

_____

_____

Are there any memorable events in the settlement's past? How did they shape the present?

_____

_____

_____

_____

THE INHABITANTS

Who is the current leader and what is their title? How long have they been in power?

_____

_____

_____

Are there any individuals or organization, either based here or not, that influence events? What do they want?

_____

_____

_____

_____

_____

_____

Are there any important individuals living here now, in the past, or who grew up here?

_____

_____

_____

Are there any monsters or creatures in or around the settlement? Describe location and past incidents.

_____

_____

_____

_____

_____

_____

_____

_____

_____

_____

_____

What species and races are here? How common are they, how are they treated/viewed/welcomed?

Species/Race Name	Species/Race Name	Species/Race Name
_____	_____	_____
How common are they?	How common are they?	How common are they?
_____	_____	_____
_____	_____	_____
How are they viewed?	How are they viewed?	How are they viewed?
_____	_____	_____
_____	_____	_____
_____	_____	_____

Species/Race Name	Species/Race Name	Species/Race Name
_____	_____	_____
How common are they?	How common are they?	How common are they?
_____	_____	_____
_____	_____	_____
How are they viewed?	How are they viewed?	How are they viewed?
_____	_____	_____
_____	_____	_____
_____	_____	_____

OTHER DETAILS

What religions are practiced here? Which ones are shunned?

_____

_____

_____

_____

_____

What monetary system is used? Does it differ from the sovereign power this might be part of?

_____

_____

What local laws exist about the use of magic or technology?

_____

_____

_____

_____

_____

_____

_____

_____

What other laws, crimes, and punishment exist here? You may have defined them in another section.

_____

_____

_____

_____

_____

_____

Are there any phenomena here? What impact do they have? Where are they located?

_____

_____

_____

_____

_____

Are there any important locations in town, such as important buildings beyond what is usually expected (like city hall)?

_____

_____

_____

_____

What festivals and holidays are unique to this location?

_____

_____

_____

_____

What education systems exist here? You may have defined them in another section.

_____

_____

_____

_____

_____

FINAL NOTES

_____

_____

_____

_____

_____

_____

_____

_____

_____

_____

_____

_____

_____

_____

_____

_____

_____

_____

_____

_____

PLACES OF INTEREST

In this section, you will create several places of interest, such as ruins, catacombs, and monuments.

PLACE OF INTEREST 1

What type of place is it?

_____

What is interesting, unique, or memorable about it

_____

_____

_____

Is it easy or difficult to find or access? Do people know where it is?

_____

_____

Is it guarded or populated by something dangerous? Is it abandoned? What is here and what danger does it pose?

_____

_____

_____

_____

_____

PLACE OF INTEREST 2

What type of place is it?

_____

What is interesting, unique, or memorable about it

_____

_____

_____

Is it easy or difficult to find or access? Do people know where it is?

_____

_____

Is it guarded or populated by something dangerous? Is it abandoned? What danger does it pose?

_____

_____

_____

_____

_____

_____

_____

_____

_____

_____

_____

PLACE OF INTEREST 3

What type of place is it?

_____

What is interesting, unique, or memorable about it

_____

_____

_____

Is it easy or difficult to find or access? Do people know where it is?

_____

_____

Is it guarded or populated by something dangerous? Is it abandoned? What is here and what danger does it pose?

_____

_____

_____

_____

_____

_____

_____

_____

_____

_____

PLACE OF INTEREST 4

What type of place is it?

_____

What is interesting, unique, or memorable about it

_____

_____

_____

Is it easy or difficult to find or access? Do people know where it is?

_____

_____

Is it guarded or populated by something dangerous? Is it abandoned? What is here and what danger does it pose?

_____

_____

_____

_____

_____

_____

_____

_____

_____

_____

WORLD HISTORY

In this section, you will create a high level world history listing the most important time frames and events. Any history for species/races, sovereign power, settlements and more should be created in their sections. Section 2 has the universal calendar, including the year designation, such as B.C. and A.D. on Earth.

Creating a history is an iterative process that brings a problem in a written workbook – the desire to squeeze another entry in between two already written down. In addition to writing in pencil, you may want to leave several blank sections in between initial entries.

For all entries, include the what, where, and when. However, the why and how are less important. The who should either be a person or a sovereign power or group – whoever is the actor or recipient of the action.

ENTRY 1

Year: _____

Event description: _____

_____

_____

_____

_____

_____

_____

_____

_____

ENTRY 2

Year: _____

Event description: _____

_____

_____

_____

_____

ENTRY 3

Year: _____

Event description: _____

_____

_____

_____

ENTRY 4

Year: _____

Event description: _____

_____

_____

_____

ENTRY 5

Year: _____

Event description: _____

_____

_____

_____

_____

_____

ENTRY 6

Year: _____

Event description: _____

_____

_____

_____

_____

ENTRY 7

Year: _____

Event description: _____

_____

_____

_____

_____

Entry 8

Year:

Event description:

Entry 9

Year:

Event description:

Entry 10

Year:

Event description:

ENTRY 11

Year:

Event description:

ENTRY 12

Year:

Event description:

ENTRY 13

Year:

Event description:

Entry 14

Year:

Event description:

Entry 15

Year:

Event description:

Entry 16

Year:

Event description:

ENTRY 17

Year: _____

Event description: _____

_____

_____

_____

_____

ENTRY 18

Year: _____

Event description: _____

_____

_____

_____

_____

ENTRY 19

Year: _____

Event description: _____

_____

_____

_____

_____

GODS AND PANTHEONS

In this section, you will create several gods in one or more pantheons.

PANTHEON 1

What is the name of this pantheon (i.e., Roman, Norse)?

_____

What is the creation myth of this pantheon? From where did the gods and all life originate?

_____

_____

_____

What is the end of times myth? Will all life and gods cease to exist or enter a new state/existence? What triggers this?

_____

_____

_____

_____

Can the gods mate and produce offspring? With only themselves, other supernatural entities, or with species/races?

_____

_____

_____

Are there lesser gods like demi-gods? What form (humanoid, dragon) is each? Who do they serve? What do they do?

Name	Name	Name
Form:	Form:	Form:
Serves:	Serves:	Serves:
Purpose/job	Purpose/job	Purpose/job
Notes	Notes	Notes

Name	Name	Name
Form:	Form:	Form:
Serves:	Serves:	Serves:
Purpose/job	Purpose/job	Purpose/job
Notes	Notes	Notes

Where do the gods dwell, generally? What buildings or places exist there?

_____

_____

_____

_____

_____

Can the gods die? How? Natural causes? A weapon? Do they know and takes steps to avoid it? What happens if one dies?

_____

_____

_____

_____

_____

Are the gods real or did people make them up?

_____

Do the gods show up and if so, how? As a vision, in person, as possession? Do they have any rules about this?

_____

_____

_____

Can the gods punish each other? Who does it? How? What is the result?

_____

_____

_____

THE GODS

Name/Title/Nicknames	Name/Title/Nicknames	Name/Title/Nicknames
God/Patron of:	God/Patron of:	God/Patron of:
Symbol:	Symbol:	Symbol:
Appearance:	Appearance:	Appearance:
Alignment: Good Evil Neutral	Alignment: Good Evil Neutral	Alignment: Good Evil Neutral
Possessions	Possessions	Possessions
Personality	Personality	Personality
Residence	Residence	Residence
Notes	Notes	Notes

Name/Title/Nicknames	Name/Title/Nicknames	Name/Title/Nicknames
God/Patron of:	God/Patron of:	God/Patron of:
Symbol:	Symbol:	Symbol:
Appearance:	Appearance:	Appearance:
Alignment: Good Evil Neutral Possessions	Alignment: Good Evil Neutral Possessions	Alignment: Good Evil Neutral Possessions
Personality	Personality	Personality
Residence	Residence	Residence
Notes	Notes	Notes

Name/Title/Nicknames	Name/Title/Nicknames	Name/Title/Nicknames
God/Patron of:	God/Patron of:	God/Patron of:
Symbol:	Symbol:	Symbol:
Appearance:	Appearance:	Appearance:
Alignment: Good Evil Neutral Possessions	Alignment: Good Evil Neutral Possessions	Alignment: Good Evil Neutral Possessions
Personality	Personality	Personality
Residence	Residence	Residence
Notes	Notes	Notes

FAMILY TREE – PANTHEON 1 NAME:

Draw the family tree in pencil. It may be best to turn the book sideways

PANTHEON 2

What is the name of this pantheon (i.e., Roman, Norse)?

_____

_____

What is the creation myth of this pantheon? From where did the gods and all life originate?

_____

_____

_____

_____

What is the end of times myth? Will all life and gods cease to exist or enter a new state/existence? What triggers this?

_____

_____

_____

_____

_____

Can the gods mate and produce offspring? With only themselves, other supernatural entities, or with species/races?

_____

_____

_____

_____

_____

_____

_____

Are there lesser gods like demi-gods? What form (humanoid, dragon) is each? Who do they serve? What do they do?

Name	Name	Name
Form:	Form:	Form:
Serves:	Serves:	Serves:
Purpose/job	Purpose/job	Purpose/job
Notes	Notes	Notes

Name	Name	Name
Form:	Form:	Form:
Serves:	Serves:	Serves:
Purpose/job	Purpose/job	Purpose/job
Notes	Notes	Notes

Where do the gods dwell, generally? What buildings or places exist there?

_____

_____

_____

_____

_____

Can the gods die? How? Natural causes? A weapon? Do they know and takes steps to avoid it? What happens if one dies?

_____

_____

_____

_____

_____

_____

Are the gods real or did people make them up?

_____

Do the gods show up and if so, how? As a vision, in person, as possession? Do they have any rules about this?

_____

_____

_____

Can the gods punish each other? Who does it? How? What is the result?

_____

_____

_____

THE GODS

Name/Title/Nicknames	Name/Title/Nicknames	Name/Title/Nicknames
God/Patron of:	God/Patron of:	God/Patron of:
Symbol:	Symbol:	Symbol:
Appearance:	Appearance:	Appearance:
Alignment: Good Evil Neutral	Alignment: Good Evil Neutral	Alignment: Good Evil Neutral
Possessions	Possessions	Possessions
Personality	Personality	Personality
Residence	Residence	Residence
Notes	Notes	Notes

Name/Title/Nicknames	Name/Title/Nicknames	Name/Title/Nicknames
God/Patron of:	God/Patron of:	God/Patron of:
Symbol:	Symbol:	Symbol:
Appearance:	Appearance:	Appearance:
Alignment: Good Evil Neutral	Alignment: Good Evil Neutral	Alignment: Good Evil Neutral
Possessions	Possessions	Possessions
Personality	Personality	Personality
Residence	Residence	Residence
Notes	Notes	Notes

Name/Title/Nicknames	Name/Title/Nicknames	Name/Title/Nicknames
God/Patron of:	God/Patron of:	God/Patron of:
Symbol:	Symbol:	Symbol:
Appearance:	Appearance:	Appearance:
Alignment: Good Evil Neutral Possessions	Alignment: Good Evil Neutral Possessions	Alignment: Good Evil Neutral Possessions
Personality	Personality	Personality
Residence	Residence	Residence
Notes	Notes	Notes

Name/Title/Nicknames	Name/Title/Nicknames	Name/Title/Nicknames
God/Patron of:	God/Patron of:	God/Patron of:
Symbol:	Symbol:	Symbol:
Appearance:	Appearance:	Appearance:
Alignment: Good Evil Neutral Possessions	Alignment: Good Evil Neutral Possessions	Alignment: Good Evil Neutral Possessions
Personality	Personality	Personality
Residence	Residence	Residence
Notes	Notes	Notes

FAMILY TREE – PANTHEON 2 NAME:

Draw the family tree in pencil. It may be best to turn the book sideways.

SPECIES AND RACES

In this section, you will create two species or races.

SPECIES/RACE 1

What is the name? Do they have nicknames?

_____

Are they a species or race?

_____

What are they famous for? What immediately comes to mind when others think of them?

_____

_____

_____

_____

What pantheon or gods do they worship?

_____

HABITAT

What terrain do they prefer to live in? What climates are they found in or avoid?

_____

_____

_____

What are their settlements like? Sprawling? Structured? Artistic? How do they feel? Are they well managed and designed?

_____

_____

_____

_____

_____

_____

What are their homes like? What materials? Do they accommodate other species? What special rooms exist?

_____

_____

_____

_____

ATTRIBUTES

Describe them. Are they humanoid? How many appendages? What impression do they create? Include typical clothing.

_____

_____

_____

_____

_____

_____

Using a scale such as 1-10 or high to low, indicate their characteristics.

Strength	Agility	Dexterity
Value	Value	Value
Notes	Notes	Notes
Constitution	Charisma	Intelligence
Value	Value	Value
Notes	Notes	Notes
Wisdom	Morale	Other
Value	Value	Value
Notes	Notes	Notes

Do they have any unusual senses or capabilities with sight, sound, smell, taste, or feel? Is it better or worse than humans?

_____

_____

_____

Do they have any sixth senses and what are the limits of them? How common is the trait?

_____

_____

_____

_____

_____

_____

How long is pregnancy? How common are twins, etc.?

_____

_____

WORLD VIEW

What is name of their language and do they have a written one? What form of writing is it?

_____

_____

What other languages do they speak, read, or write, and to what level of proficiency?

_____

_____

_____

_____

What is their overall outlook? Are they friendly, positive, hostile, suspicious, trustworthy, generally educated or not?

A species/race will have multiple cultures, but some elements may be universal, or you may be only using one culture in the work. Decide some customs exist for marriage, birth, death, divorce, greeting, and more. This workbook has more extensive sections for culture invention.

RELATIONS

How big is a typical family? Include siblings, extended family, and whether people stay in touch, live near, or don't care.

_____

_____

_____

_____

For each species, decide their typical relationship quality. Good? Hostile? Tolerant? Grudging acceptance? Kill on sight?

Species/Race Name	Species/Race Name	Species/Race Name
_____	_____	_____
Quality: _____	Quality: _____	Quality: _____
_____	_____	_____
_____	_____	_____
_____	_____	_____
_____	_____	_____
_____	_____	_____
Species/Race Name	**Species/Race Name**	**Species/Race Name**
_____	_____	_____
Quality: _____	Quality: _____	Quality: _____
_____	_____	_____
_____	_____	_____
_____	_____	_____
_____	_____	_____
_____	_____	_____

MAGIC

What is their relationship with magic? Are they afraid of it or masters?

_____

_____

_____

Are they strong with it? Incapable? Undisciplined?

_____

_____

_____

_____

_____

_____

Are they able to get training? Do they provide it? What form is it (apprentice, school)?

_____

_____

_____

_____

Are there any known incidents, good or bad, with magic or the supernatural in the past or present?

_____

_____

_____

_____

_____

_____

COMBAT

Do they avoid combat, relish it, or see it as a necessary evil?

_____

_____

_____

Do they use any specific types of armor or weapons? List them. If creating these in the "Items" section, add details there and just reference them here.

_____

_____

_____

_____

_____

Do they use any animals in their fighting such as horses, dragons, or packs of wolves?

_____

_____

_____

_____

_____

How do they fight? Orderly? Chaos? Do they follow rules or fight dirty? Do they have honor?

_____

_____

_____

_____

Do they have any special attacks or defenses?? Does it have a name? Do they train for it? How is the move done?

_____

_____

_____

What kind of training are they able to give their own people, or must they get it from another species/race?

_____

_____

What are some famous battles they've been a part of? What was their role? Did they win or lose? What effect did it have on them?

_____

_____

_____

_____

_____

_____

_____

_____

_____

NOTES

_____

_____

_____

SPECIES/RACE 2

What is the name? Do they have nicknames?

_____

Are they a species or race?

_____

What are they famous for? What immediately comes to mind when others think of them?

_____

_____

_____

_____

_____

What pantheon or gods do they worship?

_____

HABITAT

What terrain do they prefer to live in? What climates are they found in or avoid?

_____

_____

_____

What are their settlements like? Sprawling? Structured? Artistic? How do they feel? Are they well managed and designed?

_____

_____

_____

_____

_____

_____

What are their homes like? What materials? Do they accommodate other species? What special rooms exist?

_____

_____

_____

_____

_____

_____

_____

ATTRIBUTES

Describe them. Are they humanoid? How many appendages? What impression do they create? Include typical clothing.

_____

_____

_____

_____

_____

_____

_____

_____

_____

_____

_____

_____

Using a scale such as 1-10 or high to low, indicate their characteristics.

Strength	Agility	Dexterity
Value	Value	Value
Notes	Notes	Notes
Constitution	**Charisma**	**Intelligence**
Value	Value	Value
Notes	Notes	Notes
Wisdom	**Morale**	**Other**
Value	Value	Value
Notes	Notes	Notes

Do they have any unusual senses or capabilities with sight, sound, smell, taste, or feel? Is it better or worse than humans?

_____

_____

_____

_____

_____

_____

_____

_____

_____

Do they have any sixth senses and what are the limits of them? How common is the trait?

_____

_____

_____

_____

_____

How long is pregnancy? How common are twins, etc.?

_____

_____

WORLD VIEW

What is name of their language and do they have a written one? What form of writing is it?

_____

_____

What other languages do they speak, read, or write, and to what level of proficiency?

_____

_____

_____

_____

What is their overall outlook? Are they friendly, positive, hostile, suspicious, trustworthy, generally educated or not?

_____

_____

_____

_____

_____

_____

A species/race will have multiple cultures, but some elements may be universal, or you may be only using one culture in the work. Decide some customs exist for marriage, birth, death, divorce, greeting, and more. This workbook has more extensive sections for culture invention.

_____

_____

_____

_____

_____

_____

_____

_____

_____

_____

RELATIONS

How big is a typical family? Include siblings, extended family, and whether people stay in touch, live near, or don't care.

_____

_____

_____

_____

For each species, decide their typical relationship quality. Good? Hostile? Tolerant? Grudging acceptance? Kill on sight?

Species/Race Name	Species/Race Name	Species/Race Name
_____	_____	_____
Quality:	Quality:	Quality:
_____	_____	_____
_____	_____	_____
_____	_____	_____
_____	_____	_____
_____	_____	_____
Species/Race Name	**Species/Race Name**	**Species/Race Name**
_____	_____	_____
Quality:	Quality:	Quality:
_____	_____	_____
_____	_____	_____
_____	_____	_____
_____	_____	_____
_____	_____	_____

MAGIC

What is their relationship with magic? Are they afraid of it or masters?

_____

_____

_____

Are they strong with it? Incapable? Undisciplined?

_____

_____

_____

_____

_____

Are they able to get training? Do they provide it? What form is it (apprentice, school)?

_____

_____

_____

_____

Are there any known incidents, good or bad, with magic or the supernatural in the past or present?

_____

_____

_____

_____

_____

_____

COMBAT

Do they avoid combat, relish it, or see it as a necessary evil?

_____

_____

_____

Do they use any specific types of armor or weapons? List them. If creating these in the "Items" section, add details there and just reference them here.

_____

_____

_____

_____

_____

_____

Do they use any animals in their fighting such as horses, dragons, or packs of wolves?

_____

_____

_____

_____

_____

_____

How do they fight? Orderly? Chaos? Do they follow rules or fight dirty? Do they have honor?

_____

_____

_____

_____

Do they have any special attacks or defenses?? Does it have a name? Do they train for it? How is the move done?

_____

_____

_____

What kind of training are they able to give their own people, or must they get it from another species/race?

_____

_____

What are some famous battles they've been a part of? What was their role? Did they win or lose? What effect did it have on them?

_____

_____

_____

_____

_____

_____

_____

_____

NOTES

_____

_____

_____

SPECIES/RACE 3

What is the name? Do they have nicknames?

_____

Are they a species or race?

_____

What are they famous for? What immediately comes to mind when others think of them?

_____

_____

_____

_____

_____

What pantheon or gods do they worship?

_____

HABITAT

What terrain do they prefer to live in? What climates are they found in or avoid?

_____

_____

_____

What are their settlements like? Sprawling? Structured? Artistic? How do they feel? Are they well managed and designed?

_____

_____

_____

_____

_____

_____

What are their homes like? What materials? Do they accommodate other species? What special rooms exist?

_____

_____

_____

_____

_____

_____

_____

ATTRIBUTES

Describe them. Are they humanoid? How many appendages? What impression do they create? Include typical clothing.

_____

_____

_____

_____

_____

_____

_____

_____

_____

_____

_____

_____

Using a scale such as 1-10 or high to low, indicate their characteristics.

Strength	Agility	Dexterity
Value	Value	Value
Notes	Notes	Notes
Constitution	Charisma	Intelligence
Value	Value	Value
Notes	Notes	Notes
Wisdom	Morale	Other
Value	Value	Value
Notes	Notes	Notes

Do they have any unusual senses or capabilities with sight, sound, smell, taste, or feel? Is it better or worse than humans?

_____

_____

_____

Do they have any sixth senses and what are the limits of them? How common is the trait?

_____

_____

_____

_____

_____

_____

How long is pregnancy? How common are twins, etc.?

_____

_____

WORLD VIEW

What is name of their language and do they have a written one? What form of writing is it?

_____

_____

What other languages do they speak, read, or write, and to what level of proficiency?

_____

_____

_____

_____

What is their overall outlook? Are they friendly, positive, hostile, suspicious, trustworthy, generally educated or not?

_____

_____

_____

_____

_____

_____

_____

A species/race will have multiple cultures, but some elements may be universal, or you may be only using one culture in the work. Decide some customs exist for marriage, birth, death, divorce, greeting, and more. This workbook has more extensive sections for culture invention.

_____

_____

_____

_____

_____

_____

_____

_____

_____

_____

_____

RELATIONS

How big is a typical family? Include siblings, extended family, and whether people stay in touch, live near, or don't care.

_____

_____

_____

_____

For each species, decide their typical relationship quality. Good? Hostile? Tolerant? Grudging acceptance? Kill on sight?

Species/Race Name	Species/Race Name	Species/Race Name
Quality:	Quality:	Quality:
Species/Race Name	**Species/Race Name**	**Species/Race Name**
Quality:	Quality:	Quality:

MAGIC

What is their relationship with magic? Are they afraid of it or masters?

_____

_____

_____

Are they strong with it? Incapable? Undisciplined?

_____

_____

_____

_____

_____

_____

Are they able to get training? Do they provide it? What form is it (apprentice, school)?

_____

_____

_____

_____

Are there any known incidents, good or bad, with magic or the supernatural in the past or present?

_____

_____

_____

_____

_____

_____

Combat

Do they avoid combat, relish it, or see it as a necessary evil?

_____

_____

_____

Do they use any specific types of armor or weapons? List them. If creating these in the "Items" section, add details there and just reference them here.

_____

_____

_____

_____

_____

_____

Do they use any animals in their fighting such as horses, dragons, or packs of wolves?

_____

_____

_____

_____

_____

How do they fight? Orderly? Chaos? Do they follow rules or fight dirty? Do they have honor?

_____

_____

_____

_____

Do they have any special attacks or defenses?? Does it have a name? Do they train for it? How is the move done?

_____

_____

_____

What kind of training are they able to give their own people, or must they get it from another species/race?

_____

_____

What are some famous battles they've been a part of? What was their role? Did they win or lose? What effect did it have on them?

_____

_____

_____

_____

_____

_____

_____

_____

_____

NOTES

_____

_____

_____

SPECIES/RACE 4

What is the name? Do they have nicknames?

_____

Are they a species or race?

_____

What are they famous for? What immediately comes to mind when others think of them?

_____

_____

_____

_____

_____

What pantheon or gods do they worship?

_____

HABITAT

What terrain do they prefer to live in? What climates are they found in or avoid?

_____

_____

_____

What are their settlements like? Sprawling? Structured? Artistic? How do they feel? Are they well managed and designed?

_____

_____

_____

_____

_____

_____

_____

What are their homes like? What materials? Do they accommodate other species? What special rooms exist?

_____

_____

_____

_____

_____

_____

ATTRIBUTES

Describe them. Are they humanoid? How many appendages? What impression do they create? Include typical clothing.

_____

_____

_____

_____

_____

_____

_____

_____

_____

_____

_____

Using a scale such as 1-10 or high to low, indicate their characteristics.

Strength	Agility	Dexterity
Value	Value	Value
Notes	Notes	Notes
Constitution	Charisma	Intelligence
Value	Value	Value
Notes	Notes	Notes
Wisdom	Morale	Other
Value	Value	Value
Notes	Notes	Notes

Do they have any unusual senses or capabilities with sight, sound, smell, taste, or feel? Is it better or worse than humans?

_____

_____

_____

Do they have any sixth senses and what are the limits of them? How common is the trait?

_____

_____

_____

_____

_____

How long is pregnancy? How common are twins, etc.?

_____

_____

WORLD VIEW

What is name of their language and do they have a written one? What form of writing is it?

_____

_____

What other languages do they speak, read, or write, and to what level of proficiency?

_____

_____

_____

_____

What is their overall outlook? Are they friendly, positive, hostile, suspicious, trustworthy, generally educated or not?

_____

_____

_____

_____

_____

_____

_____

A species/race will have multiple cultures, but some elements may be universal, or you may be only using one culture in the work. Decide some customs exist for marriage, birth, death, divorce, greeting, and more. This workbook has more extensive sections for culture invention.

_____

_____

_____

_____

_____

_____

_____

_____

_____

_____

_____

RELATIONS

How big is a typical family? Include siblings, extended family, and whether people stay in touch, live near, or don't care.

_____

_____

_____

_____

For each species, decide their typical relationship quality. Good? Hostile? Tolerant? Grudging acceptance? Kill on sight?

Species/Race Name	Species/Race Name	Species/Race Name
_____	_____	_____
Quality:	Quality:	Quality:
_____	_____	_____
_____	_____	_____
_____	_____	_____
_____	_____	_____
_____	_____	_____
Species/Race Name	Species/Race Name	Species/Race Name
_____	_____	_____
Quality:	Quality:	Quality:
_____	_____	_____
_____	_____	_____
_____	_____	_____
_____	_____	_____

MAGIC

What is their relationship with magic? Are they afraid of it or masters?

_____

_____

_____

Are they strong with it? Incapable? Undisciplined?

_____

_____

_____

_____

_____

_____

Are they able to get training? Do they provide it? What form is it (apprentice, school)?

_____

_____

_____

_____

_____

Are there any known incidents, good or bad, with magic or the supernatural in the past or present?

_____

_____

_____

_____

_____

_____

COMBAT

Do they avoid combat, relish it, or see it as a necessary evil?

_____

_____

_____

Do they use any specific types of armor or weapons? List them. If creating these in the "Items" section, add details there and just reference them here.

_____

_____

_____

_____

_____

Do they use any animals in their fighting such as horses, dragons, or packs of wolves?

_____

_____

_____

_____

_____

How do they fight? Orderly? Chaos? Do they follow rules or fight dirty? Do they have honor?

_____

_____

_____

_____

Do they have any special attacks or defenses?? Does it have a name? Do they train for it? How is the move done?

_____

_____

_____

What kind of training are they able to give their own people, or must they get it from another species/race?

_____

_____

What are some famous battles they've been a part of? What was their role? Did they win or lose? What effect did it have on them?

_____

_____

_____

_____

_____

_____

_____

_____

Notes

_____

_____

_____

WORLD FIGURES

In this section you will create world figures like a hero, villain, and martyr.

WORLD FIGURE 1

What is the person's name and nickname(s)?

_____

_____

Why are they famous or infamous? What do people immediately think of?

_____

_____

What profession or trait defines them? Knighthood? Fighter pilot?

_____

_____

Status: are they alive, dead, imprisoned, missing?

_____

_____

What is the most recent place of residence?

_____

_____

What well-known possessions exist? Weapons, armor, and steeds are options.

_____

RELATIONSHIPS

What is the status of parents and that generation, such as aunts and uncles? Alive?

_____

_____

_____

_____

Do any children, significant others, or former lovers exist? How long did it last and end? What are they doing and what is the relationship like now?

_____

_____

_____

_____

What are relations like with each of the species/races in the setting? What is his attitude about each? Is she welcome among them? How does he treat them?

_____

_____

_____

_____

HISTORY

What sovereign power and settlement is she from?

_____

What formative events made him who he is?

_____

_____

_____

_____

How did she skills? Training? Apprenticeship? Just figured it out?

_____

_____

_____

_____

What deeds made him famous? What made him famous?

_____

_____

_____

_____

_____

_____

NOTES

_____

_____

_____

_____

_____

_____

_____

_____

_____

_____

WORLD FIGURE 2

What is the person's name and nickname(s)?

_____

_____

Why are they famous or infamous? What do people immediately think of?

_____

_____

What profession or trait defines them? Knighthood? Fighter pilot?

_____

_____

Status: are they alive, dead, imprisoned, missing?

_____

_____

What is the most recent place of residence?

_____

_____

What well-known possessions exist? Weapons, armor, and steeds are options.

_____

_____

RELATIONSHIPS

What is the status of parents and that generation, such as aunts and uncles? Alive?

_____

_____

_____

_____

Do any children, significant others, or former lovers exist? How long did it last and end? What are they doing and what is the relationship like now?

_____

_____

_____

_____

What are relations like with each of the species/races in the setting? What is his attitude about each? Is she welcome among them? How does he treat them?

_____

_____

_____

_____

HISTORY

What sovereign power and settlement is she from?

_____

What formative events made him who he is?

_____

_____

_____

_____

How did she skills? Training? Apprenticeship? Just figured it out?

_____

_____

_____

_____

_____

What deeds made him famous? What made him famous?

_____

_____

_____

_____

_____

NOTES

World Figure 3

What is the person's name and nickname(s)?

_____

_____

Why are they famous or infamous? What do people immediately think of?

_____

_____

What profession or trait defines them? Knighthood? Fighter pilot?

_____

_____

Status: are they alive, dead, imprisoned, missing?

_____

_____

What is the most recent place of residence?

_____

What well-known possessions exist? Weapons, armor, and steeds are options.

_____

_____

Relationships

What is the status of parents and that generation, such as aunts and uncles? Alive?

_____

_____

_____

_____

Do any children, significant others, or former lovers exist? How long did it last and end? What are they doing and what is the relationship like now?

_____

_____

_____

_____

What are relations like with each of the species/races in the setting? What is his attitude about each? Is she welcome among them? How does he treat them?

_____

_____

_____

_____

HISTORY

What sovereign power and settlement is she from?

_____

What formative events made him who he is?

_____

_____

_____

How did she skills? Training? Apprenticeship? Just figured it out?

_____

_____

_____

_____

What deeds made him famous? What made him famous?

_____

_____

_____

_____

_____

_____

NOTES

_____

_____

_____

_____

_____

_____

_____

_____

_____

_____

_____

_____

MONSTERS

In this section, you will create two monsters.

MONSTER 1

If the monster has a name, what is it? Does it have any nicknames?

_____

What is the monster famous for?

_____

_____

_____

What does the monster look like? Are stories of this exaggerated?

_____

_____

_____

What does the monster want? To be left alone? Hoard treasure? Food? Security? Revenge?

_____

_____

What is the monster's origin? Did someone create it or was it an accident? What happened?

_____

_____

CHARACTERISTICS

Using a scale such as 1-10 or high to low, indicate the monster's characteristics.

Strength	Agility	Dexterity
Value _____	Value _____	Value _____
Notes _____	Notes _____	Notes _____
_____	_____	_____
_____	_____	_____
Constitution	Charisma	Intelligence
Value _____	Value _____	Value _____
Notes _____	Notes _____	Notes _____
_____	_____	_____
_____	_____	_____
Wisdom	Morale	Other
Value _____	Value _____	Value _____
Notes _____	Notes _____	Notes _____
_____	_____	_____
_____	_____	_____

WORLD VIEW

What is the monster's viewpoint about itself, others, and its place in the world?

_____

_____

_____

What impact does the monster have on society? Is it seen often or rarely? Do people avoid certain behaviors to minimize interaction? How is it thought of?

_____

_____

_____

_____

_____

_____

Can the monster speak any languages? Can it be understood? Can it read?

_____

_____

_____

What habits does the monster have? Options include leaving a trail, only coming at light, displaying bodies, and more.

_____

_____

_____

What skills does the monster have?

_____

_____

_____

_____

Where does the monster live? What condition is home in? How hard is it to find?

_____

_____

What does the monster consume to stay alive? What does it avoid?

_____

_____

Can the monster reproduce? They usually can't.

_____

_____

How can the monster be killed? Is something unusual required?

_____

_____

_____

How does the monster fight? Which body parts are used? Any weapons? Is it cunning? Stealthy?

_____

_____

_____

What is this monster's relationship with different species like? Do some protect it or cooperate with it? Does someone have it guarding something? Do some want it killed or allowed to live in peace? Determine this for each species/race.

_____

_____

_____

_____

_____

Monster 2

If the monster has a name, what is it? Does it have any nicknames?

_____

_____

What is the monster famous for?

_____

_____

_____

What does the monster look like? Are stories of this exaggerated?

_____

_____

_____

What does the monster want? To be left alone? Hoard treasure? Food? Security? Revenge?

_____

_____

_____

What is the monster's origin? Did someone create it or was it an accident? What happened?

_____

_____

_____

_____

CHARACTERISTICS

Using a scale such as 1-10 or high to low, indicate the monster's characteristics.

Strength	Agility	Dexterity
Value	Value	Value
Notes	Notes	Notes
Constitution	Charisma	Intelligence
Value	Value	Value
Notes	Notes	Notes
Wisdom	Morale	Other
Value	Value	Value
Notes	Notes	Notes

WORLD VIEW

What is the monster's viewpoint about itself, others, and its place in the world?

What impact does the monster have on society? Is it seen often or rarely? Do people avoid certain behaviors to minimize interaction? How is it thought of?

_____

_____

_____

_____

_____

_____

_____

Can the monster speak any languages? Can it be understood? Can it read?

_____

_____

_____

What habits does the monster have? Options include leaving a trail, only coming at light, displaying bodies, and more.

_____

_____

_____

What skills does the monster have?

_____

_____

_____

_____

_____

Where does the monster live? What condition is home in? How hard is it to find?

_____

_____

What does the monster consume to stay alive? What does it avoid?

_____

_____

Can the monster reproduce? They usually can't.

_____

_____

How can the monster be killed? Is something unusual required?

_____

_____

_____

How does the monster fight? Which body parts are used? Any weapons? Is it cunning? Stealthy?

_____

_____

_____

What is this monster's relationship with different species like? Do some protect it or cooperate with it? Does someone have it guarding something? Do some want it killed or allowed to live in peace? Determine this for each species/race.

_____

_____

_____

_____

_____

UNDEAD

What is the undead type called? Does it have nicknames?

_____

How common are they?

_____

What does it look like? Does it appear alive or obviously dead? If a spirit, does it retain a self-image of itself as healthy and alive as if its unaware of its death?

_____

_____

_____

_____

What type of undead is it? Animal, plant, humanoid; spiritual or corporeal (with or without a soul?).

_____

What caused the first of its kind to exist? An accident? Or did someone do it on purpose? When, where, who, how, etc.

_____

_____

_____

_____

Can it make more of itself? How does it do so? How long does it take? Is there a way to resist becoming one?

_____

_____

_____

_____

Can it be destroyed for good and how? Is it sometimes only incapacitated and recovers?

_____

_____

_____

Where is it found? What are the conditions needed? It is only at night? Caves? Graveyards?

_____

_____

_____

Is it solitary or a pack animal? Can they work together strategically and at what level (random, like wolves, or people)?

_____

_____

_____

What does it want? What happens if the goal is achieved?

_____

_____

_____

How does it fight? Can it use weapons and armor? What cannot hurt it and what can?

_____

_____

_____

What can it do? How fast, strong, smart is it? Can it read/write? Can it do magic, move through walls, or compel humans?

_____

_____

_____

CULTURES

.

In this section, you will create several cultures. Remember that a species should not have a single culture. You should invent the cultures that you need for the story. Each species/race needs one, and each socio-economic status encountered.

CULTURE 1

What is the name of this culture? It can be one just for your files and not mentioned by those in the setting.

_____

_____

What is the scope of the culture? A sovereign power, region, settlement, species/race, or subgroup like royalty?

_____

_____

Circle the morals and values of this culture

Acceptance	Generosity	Politeness
Compassion	Gratitude	Respect
Cooperation	Honesty	Responsibility
Courage	Integrity	Self-control
Dignity	Kindness	Tolerance
Equality	Justice	Trustworthiness
Fairness	Perseverance	

Invent several expressions that are made when greeting peers and superiors. What physical behaviors accompany these?

_____

_____

_____

How are birthdays celebrated? What ceremonies exist? Are there festivals they participate in?

_____

_____

_____

_____

_____

What fables/stories (and their characters or objects) exist? What lesson do they teach?

_____

_____

_____

_____

What impression do buildings give? What colors and materials dominate? Is there order or chaos?

_____

_____

_____

_____

_____

_____

_____

_____

_____

THE BODY

How is eye contact handled? Is deference shown? Is a gaze challenging?

For body language, do people move stiffly, relaxed, reserved, hunched over, sexy?

How is hair worn by each gender, child, and professions of importance? Do circumstances change this?

Do people modify bodies with piercings, tattoos, or implants? How commonly?

What gestures are common and what do they mean?

_____

_____

_____

_____

_____

_____

_____

How do people wear their clothes? What accessories are so common that they're part of typical dress?

_____

_____

_____

_____

_____

_____

_____

_____

_____

_____

_____

DAILY LIFE

For dining, what etiquette is followed? Do people talk with their mouth full? Is dining formal/informal? Are there multiple forks and spoons? Do people double dip? Is the mouth wiped on their sleeve, a napkin, or a tablecloth?

_____

_____

_____

_____

_____

_____

_____

How often do people bathe? Do they do so alone? Is hot water an option? Do they bathe in a river or a private tub? Is bath water used by multiple people?

_____

_____

_____

_____

_____

_____

Do people sleep alone? Do married people share a bed? What do people wear?

_____

_____

_____

_____

_____

What is the work week? How many hours a day, per week? Is there a siesta? Are people paid for days off and holidays?

_____

_____

_____

_____

_____

_____

Is public transportation available and if so, what is it, how good is it, and what's the cost? What is its reputation?

_____

_____

_____

_____

_____

What do people do for fun?

_____

_____

_____

_____

_____

CULTURE 2

What is the name of this culture? It can be one just for your files and not mentioned by those in the setting.

_____

_____

What is the scope of the culture? A sovereign power, region, settlement, species/race, or subgroup like royalty?

_____

_____

Circle the morals and values of this culture

Acceptance	Generosity	Politeness
Compassion	Gratitude	Respect
Cooperation	Honesty	Responsibility
Courage	Integrity	Self-control
Dignity	Kindness	Tolerance
Equality	Justice	Trustworthiness
Fairness	Perseverance	

Invent several expressions that are made when greeting peers and superiors. What physical behaviors accompany these?

_____

_____

_____

How are birthdays celebrated? What ceremonies exist? Are there festivals they participate in?

_____

_____

_____

_____

_____

_____

What fables/stories (and their characters or objects) exist? What lesson do they teach?

_____

_____

_____

_____

_____

_____

What impression do buildings give? What colors and materials dominate? Is there order or chaos?

_____

_____

_____

_____

_____

_____

_____

_____

_____

THE BODY

How is eye contact handled? Is deference shown? Is a gaze challenging?

For body language, do people move stiffly, relaxed, reserved, hunched over, sexy?

How is hair worn by each gender, child, and professions of importance? Do circumstances change this?

Do people modify bodies with piercings, tattoos, or implants? How commonly?

What gestures are common and what do they mean?

_____

_____

_____

_____

_____

_____

_____

How do people wear their clothes? What accessories are so common that they're part of typical dress?

_____

_____

_____

_____

_____

_____

_____

_____

_____

_____

_____

DAILY LIFE

For dining, what etiquette is followed? Do people talk with their mouth full? Is dining formal/informal? Are there multiple forks and spoons? Do people double dip? Is the mouth wiped on their sleeve, a napkin, or a tablecloth?

_____

_____

_____

_____

_____

_____

_____

_____

How often do people bathe? Do they do so alone? Is hot water an option? Do they bathe in a river or a private tub? Is bath water used by multiple people?

_____

_____

_____

_____

_____

_____

_____

_____

Do people sleep alone? Do married people share a bed? What do people wear?

_____

_____

What is the work week? How many hours a day, per week? Is there a siesta? Are people paid for days off and holidays?

Is public transportation available and if so, what is it, how good is it, and what's the cost? What is its reputation?

What do people do for fun?

ORGANIZATIONS

In this section, you will create several organizations.

ORGANIZATION 1

What is the name of this organization?

_____

Is the group considered good, evil, or more complicated? For which do you intend to use it?

_____

_____

_____

What are the symbols and colors associated with it? What do they mean?

_____

_____

_____

_____

For what is the organization famous?

_____

_____

_____

_____

TRAITS

Are there guiding ideas that this group follows, such as the strong shall not prey upon the weak? What is the group's philosophy and how does this affect their actions?

What does this group want to achieve? Control objects? Control access to land or who's in control of it? Does it want power to achieve something? How close are they to achieving the goal(s)?

Where are they based and where do they operate? What sort of headquarters do they have, if any? Is it hidden or in plain sight? Is there anything special inside it? Is it guarded and if so, by what?

_____

_____

_____

Is the group still operating, defunct, or once gone and being resurrected?

_____

_____

_____

Does the group own any shared resources, like ships, a castle, or supernatural items? How is their usage managed?

_____

_____

_____

_____

RELATIONSHIPS

How do they get along with each species or race in the setting? Do they accept or restrict some from joining?

_____

_____

_____

_____

_____

_____

_____

_____

Who are their enemies? This can be individuals, other organizations, and sovereign powers.

_____

_____

_____

_____

_____

Who are their friends?

_____

_____

_____

_____

_____

Who leads the group? How are they chosen? How does power change hands?

_____

_____

_____

_____

_____

What requirements must members meet to join and remain?

_____

_____

_____

_____

_____

_____

Can members leave the organization? What must be done?

_____

_____

_____

Are any members especially important? Why?

_____

_____

_____

HISTORY

What deeds has the group done? Did they get the desired outcome? Why or why not? What repercussions were they?

_____

_____

_____

_____

What is the group's history? When and how did they form?

_____

_____

ORGANIZATION 2

What is the name of this organization?

_____

Is the group considered good, evil, or more complicated? For which do you intend to use it?

_____

_____

_____

What are the symbols and colors associated with it? What do they mean?

_____

_____

_____

_____

For what is the organization famous?

_____

_____

_____

_____

TRAITS

Are there guiding ideas that this group follows, such as the strong shall not prey upon the weak? What is the group's philosophy and how does this affect their actions?

_____

_____

_____

———————————————————————————————————

———————————————————————————————————

———————————————————————————————————

———————————————————————————————————

———————————————————————————————————

What does this group want to achieve? Control objects? Control access to land or who's in control of it? Does it want power to achieve something? How close are they to achieving the goal(s)?

———————————————————————————————————

———————————————————————————————————

———————————————————————————————————

———————————————————————————————————

———————————————————————————————————

———————————————————————————————————

Where are they based and where do they operate? What sort of headquarters do they have, if any? Is it hidden or in plain sight? Is there anything special inside it? Is it guarded and if so, by what?

———————————————————————————————————

———————————————————————————————————

———————————————————————————————————

———————————————————————————————————

———————————————————————————————————

———————————————————————————————————

Is the group still operating, defunct, or once gone and being resurrected?

———————————————————————————————————

———————————————————————————————————

_____

_____

Does the group own any shared resources, like ships, a castle, or supernatural items? How is their usage managed?

_____

_____

_____

RELATIONSHIPS

How do they get along with each species or race in the setting? Do they accept or restrict some from joining?

_____

_____

_____

_____

_____

_____

_____

Who are their enemies? This can be individuals, other organizations, and sovereign powers.

_____

_____

_____

_____

_____

Who are their friends?

_____

_____

_____

_____

_____

Who leads the group? How are they chosen? How does power change hands?

_____

_____

_____

_____

_____

What requirements must members meet to join and remain?

_____

_____

_____

_____

_____

Can members leave the organization? What must be done?

_____

_____

_____

Are any members especially important? Why?

_____

_____

_____

_____

_____

HISTORY

What deeds has the group done? Did they get the desired outcome? Why or why not? What repercussions were they?

_____

_____

_____

_____

_____

What is the group's history? When and how did they form?

_____

_____

_____

_____

_____

_____

_____

_____

_____

ARMED FORCES

Most world builders only need standard militaries like the army, navy, air/space force, and marines. This section assumes you may want to invent something unique and allows the creation of one.

What is the name of the military force? Does it have nicknames?

_____

_____

_____

_____

What are the symbols and colors? What do they mean?

_____

_____

_____

_____

What is the group famous for?

_____

_____

_____

_____

_____

_____

What is the basic description of what this group is or does?

_____

_____

_____

_____

_____

_____

_____

LOCATIONS

On what sort of terrain can they operate Circle all that apply

Grasslands   Desserts   Mountains

Forests Types: **Wetlands Types**   Hills
Forest Woodland Savannah Jungle   Fens Bogs Marshes Swamps

                                                                      Deep water   Shallow Water

Notes on terrains:

_____

_____

_____

_____

_____

Are there any locations they revere, fear, or where something notable happened? Do they have special buildings that cater to their needs and which are found in many locations?

_____

_____

_____

HISTORY

WORLD VIEW

What is their place in society? Do people respect or fear them, or take them for granted? Are they honored with holidays? Do they get special discounts at stores?

_____

_____

_____

_____

_____

_____

_____

What languages are they required to speak, read, and write?

_____

_____

_____

_____

What customs exist among them? These might be greetings, battle oaths, salutes, and more.

_____

_____

_____

_____

_____

Relationships

Is there a region (including sovereign powers), city, or place where they well received or hated?

_____

_____

_____

_____

_____

Those Who Serve

Who is in charge of the group? They could have a rank or title, but in your story/game, you may wish to indicate a person.

_____

_____

_____

What species or races are accepted, rejected, or in positions of power, typically?

_____

_____

_____

_____

For every species/race in the setting, work out how they get along and view each other.

_____

_____

_____

_____

_____

_____

_____

_____

_____

_____

_____

_____

_____

How do they get along with other armed forces in the setting? Is there cooperation, competition, reluctant acceptance?

_____

_____

_____

_____

_____

Are there any important characters or famous members in the past or present? Name them, the reason, and their deed.

_____

_____

_____

_____

_____

_____

_____

_____

_____

What skills or traits must they have before being accepted into training?

_____

_____

_____

What symbols of acceptance exist? These could be pins, weapons, armors, tattoos, and more.

_____

_____

_____

What ranks exist?

_____

_____

_____

_____

_____

_____

ARMS

What weapons do they typically use?

_____

_____

_____

_____

What kind of armors are used most often or required?

_____

_____

_____

COMBAT

Invent some details on how they fight, including any back up skill like hand-to-hand fighting when disarmed. What are they not good at defending against (think a specific martial arts style)?

_____

_____

_____

_____

Do they have any special attacks or defenses?

_____

_____

_____

_____

Do they participate in wars? How are they typically used?

_____

_____

_____

_____

Do they participate in duels or tournaments?

_____

_____

_____

_____

Have they done any famous or important missions? Describe what happened, its affect on them, and more.

_____

_____

_____

_____

_____

_____

Do they have any major accomplishments or discoveries?

_____

_____

_____

RELIGIONS

In this section, you will create one religion. Most stories or games don't need more than that in detail.

What is the name of this religion? Are there nicknames?

_____

What are the symbols and associated colors? What do they represent?

_____

_____

_____

_____

_____

For what is the religion famous? What immediately comes to mind when people think of it?

_____

_____

_____

_____

_____

_____

HISTORY

How long ago was the religion formed?

_____

What event led to the religion forming? This is often a prophet receiving the word of the god. Invent details such as the prophet's name, location of the event, and items present (these often become symbols).

_____

_____

_____

_____

_____

_____

_____

_____

_____

_____

_____

_____

_____

_____

WORLD VIEW

How often must they pray at home or at church? Is it formal? Are any materials or positions required (kneeling)?

_____

_____

_____

_____

Every religion will have an annual holiday and possibly events that take place regularly, such as once a week, month, or seasons. List some events here and their significance.

_____

_____

_____

_____

_____

_____

_____

_____

How do various kinds of sovereign powers (kingdoms, dictatorships) view them? Good or bad? Are they influential?

_____

_____

_____

_____

_____

Invent several holy sites, their significance, how often they should be visited, and what people must do once there.

SITE 1

_____

_____

_____

_____

_____

SITE 2

_____

_____

_____

_____

_____

SITE 3

_____

_____

_____

_____

_____

_____

_____

Do they do outreach like missionary work? How is this viewed?

_____

_____

_____

_____

What language is the official one? Are priests expected to know others? Are any forbidden?

_____

_____

_____

_____

What is the afterlife like? Does it have a name? How do people earn their spot there (or keep it)? How do they get there?

_____

_____

_____

_____

_____

_____

_____

_____

_____

_____

_____

RELATIONSHIPS

What is the quality of their relationships with each species/race like?

Species/Race Name	Species/Race Name	Species/Race Name
Quality:	Quality:	Quality:
Species/Race Name	Species/Race Name	Species/Race Name
Quality:	Quality:	Quality:

How is the clergy or practitioners viewed by the military? Is it favorable? Are they included?

_____

_____

_____

_____

Are there other religions that they have an unusually good or bad relationship with?

_____

_____

_____

_____

COMBAT

Are they allowed t participate in combat, personally wielding a weapon? Are they allowed to wear armor?

_____

_____

_____

_____

What preferred weapons and armor exist? Is anything forbidden?

_____

_____

_____

_____

NOTES

_____

_____

_____

_____

_____

THE SUPERNATURAL

In this section, you will create supernatural phenomena and places.

PHENOMENA 1

What is the name of it? Does it have a nickname?

_____

What type is it? Magic, radiation, divine power, or something else

_____

How often can this be used or encountered? Are those who harness it fatigued?

_____

_____

_____

Where is it located? Is there a type of place where it is found? What conditions must exist?

_____

_____

_____

_____

_____

PROPERTIES

What does it look like? Is it visible or only with aided sight? Must conditions be met for it to appear?

_____

_____

_____

_____

What does it feel like if it can be felt at all? This includes temperature range and whether it gives off heat, cold, or nothing. If the energy can be touched or sensed, what happens to flesh or senses? Is anything heightened or muted?

_____

_____

_____

_____

How long does it last when encountered? Does it have phases, like a volcano?

_____

_____

_____

Is the intensity constant or in a state of flux?

_____

_____

HISTORY

Deciding its origins is optional as natural phenomena need no explanation, but did something cause this?

_____

_____

Invent a few incidents that have happened with this energy, including when it was first discovered, first contained, or first used as a weapon, especially if these went wrong or had significant impact on events of the time.

_____

_____

_____

_____

_____

_____

USAGE

Do people harness this energy for anything, or would they like to? Using it to power ship engines comes to mind. Can it be weaponized?

_____

_____

_____

_____

_____

Can it be controlled? Is a device needed? Is there a limit on that control? What happens when control of it is lost?

_____

_____

_____

_____

_____

_____

_____

_____

Phenomena 2

What is the name of it? Does it have a nickname?

_____

What type is it? Magic, radiation, divine power, or something else

_____

How often can this be used or encountered? Are those who harness it fatigued?

_____

_____

Where is it located? Is there a type of place where it is found? What conditions must exist?

_____

_____

_____

_____

Properties

What does it look like? Is it visible or only with aided sight? Must conditions be met for it to appear?

_____

_____

_____

_____

_____

What does it feel like if it can be felt at all? This includes temperature range and whether it gives off heat, cold, or nothing. If the energy can be touched or sensed, what happens to flesh or senses? Is anything heightened or muted?

_____

_____

_____

_____

How long does it last when encountered? Does it have phases, like a volcano?

_____

_____

_____

Is the intensity constant or in a state of flux?

_____

_____

HISTORY

Deciding its origins is optional as natural phenomena need no explanation, but did something cause this?

_____

_____

Invent a few incidents that have happened with this energy, including when it was first discovered, first contained, or first used as a weapon, especially if these went wrong or had significant impact on events of the time.

_____

_____

_____

_____

_____

USAGE

Do people harness this energy for anything, or would they like to? Using it to power ship engines comes to mind. Can it be weaponized?

———————————————————————————

———————————————————————————

———————————————————————————

———————————————————————————

Can it be controlled? Is a device needed? Is there a limit on that control? What happens when control of it is lost?

———————————————————————————

———————————————————————————

———————————————————————————

———————————————————————————

———————————————————————————

———————————————————————————

———————————————————————————

———————————————————————————

———————————————————————————

———————————————————————————

———————————————————————————

SUPERNATURAL PLACE

What is the name of this place? Does it have a nickname?

_____

_____

Where is it located? On a physical planet or another reality?

_____

_____

How do people reach it? Are there doorways or portals? Is a device needed? Is it guarded or available at certain times?

_____

_____

_____

_____

_____

Are there regions inside, like territories or features (such as a forest)? Such regions might be named for phenomena there.

_____

_____

_____

_____

_____

Are there any settlements inside? Do they stay in one place or move? What is their attitude about travelers arriving?

_____

_____

_____

_____

_____

Do any buildings exist? Are some holy ground? Do they harbor bad things? Are they a trap?

_____

_____

_____

_____

_____

_____

INHABITANTS

Who rules this land? Is that contested and by whom? What powers do they have?

_____

_____

_____

_____

_____

_____

Is there a horde of any creature here? What attracts them to visitors? Where do they live? How can they be destroyed?

_____

_____

_____

_____

_____

Has any species/race taken up residence? How many? Is it voluntary? Is anyone famous here, maybe unknowingly?

_____

_____

_____

_____

_____

Are there any animals specific to here? Are they corrupted? Did they wander in from the normal world?

_____

_____

_____

HISTORY

Have any important events taken place in here before? What was the result?

_____

_____

_____

How did this land originate? Was it on purpose or an accident?

_____

_____

_____

_____

Will this place cease to exist one day? When and how will it happen? Must a condition be met?

_____

_____

_____

_____

_____

Are there any stories about this place? Are they true or not?

_____

_____

_____

_____

_____

_____

_____

_____

_____

_____

_____

_____

_____

MAGIC SYSTEM AND SPELLS

In this section, you will create a magic system and spells. Some consider a system to be only necromancy, for example, while others might consider a system to include both necromancy and witchcraft, as two examples. This section assumes the former case, so if you wanted to define necromancy, you would do so here.

Does the overall magic system have a name or nickname?

_____

_____

Does it have a symbol? What does it mean? Colors are less frequent but can also be done.

_____

_____

For what is the magic system or its practitioners famous? What immediately comes to mind?

_____

_____

_____

_____

_____

DESCRIPTION

At a high level, what can practitioners do and not do?

_____

_____

_____

_____

_____

_____

_____

_____

_____

What is the source of magic? The gods or the universe? Who made it possible?

_____

_____

When the spellcaster is summoning power, where does it come from? People? The environment?

_____

_____

What laws of magic govern usage? Can people perform this type and another? Must anything happen first?

_____

_____

_____

_____

How common is this type of magic and its practitioners?

_____

_____

_____

_____

What is the cost of performing magic? What toll does it take on caster and environment?

_____

_____

_____

_____

_____

_____

Are spells needed to do it or can it be done by force of will?

_____

_____

_____

_____

What happens when an attempt at using magic fails?

_____

_____

_____

_____

_____

_____

Are there any special sites, like training centers, or places where magic doesn't work or behaves differently?

_____

_____

_____

_____

_____

_____

Invent famous practitioners from the past and their deeds and the impacts.

_____

_____

_____

_____

_____

_____

_____

_____

_____

_____

_____

WORLD VIEW

How do most societies view them? Are they beneficial or harmful? Celebrated or shunned? Does family reject them?

_____

_____

_____

_____

_____

_____

Is there a magic language, or another unique one, that they speak, read, and write? What is it called? Can others learn it or is magic talent and training required?

_____

_____

_____

_____

_____

Are their customary behaviors like greetings, farewells, or deference shown to or by them?

_____

_____

_____

_____

_____

PRACTITIONERS

Is there a governing body where practices are codified? Who is the head of this and how is such a person chosen?

Is there a species, race, gender, or other characteristic that influences who becomes a practitioner? What percentage of each does this? What "walk of life" are they from?

Are any species/races forbidden or rare as a practitioner? Why?

Are any species/races forbidden or common as a practitioner? Why?

_____

_____

_____

_____

_____

_____

_____

_____

Are there groups, including military, with whom they have an ongoing relationship? This could be as allies or enemies.

_____

_____

_____

_____

_____

_____

_____

_____

_____

_____

BECOMING ONE

How does someone acquire the talent and/or ability? Can they lose it and how?

_____

_____

_____

_____

_____

What kind of training is available? Formal schooling, an apprenticeship? How easy is it to get training? Is it expensive?

_____

_____

_____

_____

_____

_____

_____

_____

_____

_____

Once accepted as a wizard by a formal body, are there any signs of acceptance, like a pin or robe?

_____

_____

_____

Do any ranks exist within the magic system? The ranks might have skills and powers associated with them.

_____

_____

_____

_____

_____

_____

_____

_____

Are they allowed to use weapons or armor? What restrictions exist? Are laws of magic causing that or laws of "mankind?"

_____

_____

_____

_____

_____

Are they part of any military group?

_____

_____

_____

_____

_____

_____

In this section, you will create spells in this magic system. Focus on spells that are of use to you or characters.

To cast the spell, what is required? For the **words**, Are any words needed? What are they in English? What are they in the language of magic? Are they controlling what happens, summoning power, or something else?

For **gestures**, what gestures must they make to cast it? What purpose do they serve? Can the spell be done without them and if so, what impact does that have?

For **ingredients**, what materials are needed and in what quantity? Define how rare they are and how easy to carry or how something frequently is (such as a vial). Create this like a recipe, with instructions on the order to do everything in and how to handle something, such as rubbing it between fingers, snapping it, throwing it, etc. Be more elaborate if this is about creating a potion or item, for example, rather than a live spell done in battle where speed matters

For **difficulty**, how hard is the spell to cast? What skill or rank must the caster have achieved?

For **duration**, how long does the spell last? How long does it take to cast? Attack spells should be quick. There isn't necessarily a correlation between difficulty and duration to cast, but complexity is often seen as requiring more words, gestures, and ingredients.

For **range**, how far from the caster does the spell take effect and for what distance or radius? How close or far must they be from the target

For **cost**, what effect does this spell have on the caster? Fatigue? Memory loss? How does the caster feel about the prospect of casting it (will they be successful? Is the cost of casting it acceptable?)? Do they dread it or look forward to it?

For **description**, write a basic idea of what the spell does, how, and under what circumstances it can be cast or be effective. What is the spell's reputation?

GENERAL NOTES

_____

_____

_____

_____

_____

_____

_____

Spell Name:

_____

Casting

Words:

_____

Gestures:

_____

_____

Ingredients:

_____

_____

_____

_____

Difficulty

_____

Duration

_____

_____

Range

_____

_____

Cost

_____

_____

Description

_____

_____

_____

_____

_____

_____

_____

_____

_____

_____

_____

_____

_____

_____

_____

_____

_____

Spell Name:

_____

Casting

Words:

_____

Gestures:

_____

_____

Ingredients:

_____

_____

_____

_____

Difficulty

_____

Duration

_____

_____

Range

_____

_____

Cost

_____

_____

Description

_____

_____

_____

_____

_____

_____

_____

_____

_____

_____

_____

_____

_____

_____

_____

_____

Spell Name:

_____

Casting

Words:

_____

Gestures:

_____

_____

Ingredients:

_____

_____

_____

Difficulty

_____

Duration

_____

_____

Range

_____

_____

Cost

_____

_____

Description

_____

_____

_____

_____

_____

_____

_____

_____

_____

_____

_____

_____

_____

_____

Spell Name:

_____

Casting

Words:

_____

_____

Gestures:

_____

_____

Ingredients:

_____

_____

_____

_____

Difficulty

_____

Duration

_____

_____

Range

_____

_____

Cost

_____

_____

Description

_____

_____

_____

_____

_____

_____

_____

_____

_____

_____

_____

_____

_____

_____

_____

_____

Spell Name:

_____

Casting

Words:

_____

_____

Gestures:

_____

_____

Ingredients:

_____

_____

_____

Difficulty

_____

Duration

_____

_____

Range

_____

_____

Cost

_____

_____

Description

_____

_____

_____

_____

_____

_____

_____

_____

_____

_____

_____

_____

_____

_____

_____

_____

Spell Name:

Casting

Words:

Gestures:

Ingredients:

Difficulty

Duration

Range

Cost

Description

Spell Name:

_____

Casting

Words:

_____

_____

Gestures:

_____

_____

Ingredients:

_____

_____

_____

_____

Difficulty

_____

Duration

_____

_____

Range

_____

_____

Cost

_____

_____

Description

_____

_____

_____

_____

_____

_____

_____

_____

_____

_____

_____

_____

_____

_____

_____

Spell Name:

_____

Casting

Words:

_____

_____

Gestures:

_____

_____

Ingredients:

_____

_____

_____

_____

Difficulty

_____

Duration

_____

_____

Range

_____

_____

Cost

_____

_____

Description

_____

_____

_____

_____

_____

_____

_____

_____

_____

_____

_____

_____

_____

_____

_____

_____

_____

Spell Name:

Casting

Words:

Gestures:

Ingredients:

Difficulty

Duration

Range

Cost

Description

Spell Name:

_____

Casting

Words:

_____

_____

Gestures:

_____

_____

Ingredients:

_____

_____

_____

_____

Difficulty

_____

Duration

_____

_____

Range

_____

_____

Cost

_____

_____

Description

_____

_____

_____

_____

_____

_____

_____

_____

_____

_____

_____

_____

_____

_____

_____

_____

_____

Spell Name:

_____

Casting

Words:

_____

_____

Gestures:

_____

_____

Ingredients:

_____

_____

_____

_____

Difficulty

_____

Duration

_____

_____

Range

_____

_____

Cost

_____

_____

Description

_____

_____

_____

_____

_____

_____

_____

_____

_____

_____

_____

_____

_____

_____

_____

_____

_____

Spell Name:

_____

Casting

Words:

_____

_____

Gestures:

_____

_____

Ingredients:

_____

_____

_____

_____

Difficulty

_____

Duration

_____

_____

Range

_____

_____

Cost

_____

_____

Description

_____

_____

_____

_____

_____

_____

_____

_____

_____

_____

_____

_____

_____

_____

_____

_____

_____

MONETARY SYSTEMS

In this section, you will determine one or more monetary systems. These will vary across sovereign powers but can also be somewhat universal, used in multiple places.

CURRENCY 1

Name this currency for your reference, to distinguish it from others you may invent.

Is the currency a unit of weight or value? A unit of weight means the amount of gold, for example, determines the value. A unit of value means the material is not relevant because the value is printed or stamped upon it, as with paper bills. If a unit of value, what is backing it, a sovereign power, settlement, or another body?

Is money coins, gems, bills, or credits? Is it made from metal or gems? What does the money look and feel like? Do coins have milling around the edges?

Determine the scale. Example:

Material	Equivalent	Earth. Equivalent
1 iron	1 cent	1 penny
10 iron	1 copper	$1
10 coppers	1 silver	$10
10 silvers	1 gold	$100
10 gold	1 platinum	$1000

Material	Equivalent	Earth. Equivalent

NOTES

CURRENCY 2

Name this currency for your reference, to distinguish it from others you may invent.

_____

Is the currency a unit of weight or value? A unit of weight means the amount of gold, for example, determines the value. A unit of value means the material is not relevant because the value is printed or stamped upon it, as with paper bills. If a unit of value, what is backing it, a sovereign power, settlement, or another body?

_____

_____

_____

_____

_____

Is money coins, gems, bills, or credits? Is it made from metal or gems? What does the money look and feel like? Do coins have milling around the edges?

_____

_____

_____

_____

_____

_____

_____

_____

Determine the scale. Example:

Material	Equivalent	Earth. Equivalent
1 iron	1 cent	1 penny
10 iron	1 copper	$1
10 coppers	1 silver	$10
10 silvers	1 gold	$100
10 gold	1 platinum	$1000

Material	Equivalent	Earth. Equivalent

NOTES

_____

_____

_____

_____

_____

_____

_____

_____

ITEMS

In this section, you will create a number of unique or noteworthy items that exist in the setting. The type or form means weapon, armor, device, etc., and what type, for example, such as sword or helmet. Note if qualifications are needed before someone can use it, such as being a wizard to use a magic item.

Type/form:	Type/form:	Type/form:
Original Owner	Original Owner	Original Owner
Current Possessor/Location	Current Possessor/Location	Current Possessor/Location
Creator	Creator	Creator
Magical? Yes No	Magical? Yes No	Magical? Yes No
Description	Description	Description
History	History	History
Notes	Notes	Notes

Type/form:

_____

Original Owner

_____

Current Possessor/Location

_____

Creator

_____

Magical?   Yes   No

Description

_____
_____
_____
_____

History

_____
_____
_____
_____

Notes

_____
_____
_____
_____
_____
_____
_____
_____

Type/form:

_____

Original Owner

_____

Current Possessor/Location

_____

Creator

_____

Magical?   Yes   No

Description

_____
_____
_____
_____

History

_____
_____
_____
_____

Notes

_____
_____
_____
_____
_____
_____
_____
_____

Type/form:

_____

Original Owner

_____

Current Possessor/Location

_____

Creator

_____

Magical?   Yes   No

Description

_____
_____
_____
_____

History

_____
_____
_____
_____

Notes

_____
_____
_____
_____
_____
_____
_____
_____

Type/form: _____

Original Owner

_____

Current Possessor/Location

_____

Creator

_____

Magical?   Yes   No

Description

_____

_____

_____

_____

History

_____

_____

_____

_____

Notes

_____

_____

_____

_____

_____

_____

_____

_____

Type/form: _____

Original Owner

_____

Current Possessor/Location

_____

Creator

_____

Magical?   Yes   No

Description

_____

_____

_____

_____

History

_____

_____

_____

_____

Notes

_____

_____

_____

_____

_____

_____

_____

_____

Type/form: _____

Original Owner

_____

Current Possessor/Location

_____

Creator

_____

Magical?   Yes   No

Description

_____

_____

_____

_____

History

_____

_____

_____

_____

Notes

_____

_____

_____

_____

_____

_____

_____

_____

Type/form:	Type/form:	Type/form:
Original Owner	Original Owner	Original Owner
Current Possessor/Location	Current Possessor/Location	Current Possessor/Location
Creator	Creator	Creator
Magical?　Yes　No Description	Magical?　Yes　No Description	Magical?　Yes　No Description
History	History	History
Notes	Notes	Notes

NAMES

In this section, you will invent names of people, places, and things, organized by species/races.

For species/race: _____

People	Places	Things
_____	_____	_____
_____	_____	_____
_____	_____	_____
_____	_____	_____
_____	_____	_____
_____	_____	_____
_____	_____	_____
_____	_____	_____
_____	_____	_____
_____	_____	_____
_____	_____	_____
_____	_____	_____
_____	_____	_____
_____	_____	_____
_____	_____	_____
_____	_____	_____
_____	_____	_____
_____	_____	_____

For species/race: _____

People	Places	Things
_____	_____	_____
_____	_____	_____
_____	_____	_____
_____	_____	_____
_____	_____	_____
_____	_____	_____
_____	_____	_____
_____	_____	_____
_____	_____	_____
_____	_____	_____
_____	_____	_____
_____	_____	_____
_____	_____	_____
_____	_____	_____
_____	_____	_____
_____	_____	_____
_____	_____	_____
_____	_____	_____
_____	_____	_____
_____	_____	_____
_____	_____	_____
_____	_____	_____
_____	_____	_____

For species/race: _____

People	Places	Things
_____	_____	_____
_____	_____	_____
_____	_____	_____
_____	_____	_____
_____	_____	_____
_____	_____	_____
_____	_____	_____
_____	_____	_____
_____	_____	_____
_____	_____	_____
_____	_____	_____
_____	_____	_____
_____	_____	_____
_____	_____	_____
_____	_____	_____
_____	_____	_____
_____	_____	_____
_____	_____	_____
_____	_____	_____
_____	_____	_____
_____	_____	_____
_____	_____	_____
_____	_____	_____
_____	_____	_____

For species/race: _____

People	Places	Things
_____	_____	_____
_____	_____	_____
_____	_____	_____
_____	_____	_____
_____	_____	_____
_____	_____	_____
_____	_____	_____
_____	_____	_____
_____	_____	_____
_____	_____	_____
_____	_____	_____
_____	_____	_____
_____	_____	_____
_____	_____	_____
_____	_____	_____
_____	_____	_____
_____	_____	_____
_____	_____	_____
_____	_____	_____
_____	_____	_____
_____	_____	_____
_____	_____	_____
_____	_____	_____
_____	_____	_____

GAMES AND SPORTS

In this section, you will create a unique game or sport for the setting.

What is the game's name and nicknames?

_____

_____

Is there an Earth equivalent or two? Basing on it known games with alternations makes it easier to invent.

_____

_____

_____

What type of game or sport is it? Tabletop, court field? Do professional leagues exist?

_____

_____

_____

_____

Are there teams? How many players per team are what are their roles/positions?

_____

_____

_____

_____

_____

_____

_____

What skills do players need?

_____

_____

_____

_____

_____

What sort of training, knowledge, or experience is required?

_____

_____

_____

Are species or genders (or anyone else) allowed or forbidden? What social classes play this? Do the elite only watch?

_____

_____

_____

_____

GAME PLAY

What are the rules?

_____

_____

_____

_____

_____

_____

_____

_____

_____

_____

_____

_____

_____

_____

What items are needed? Balls, baskets, bats, cards, rings, dice? Is a field or court needed and how is it marked? What equipment do players wear or use?

_____

_____

_____

_____

_____

How many umpires exist and how good do they tend to be?

_____

_____

_____

_____

_____

How are penalties caused? Are there different levels of infraction? Can one be expelled over them?

_____

_____

_____

_____

How is victory achieved?

_____

_____

_____

_____

Do tournaments exist?

_____

_____

_____

_____

_____

SCORING

How is scoring handled?

Action:	Points Scored
Action:	Points Scored
Action:	Points Scored
Action:	Points Scored
Action:	Points Scored
Action:	Points Scored
Action:	Points Scored
Action:	Points Scored

LEGAL SYSTEMS

In this section, you will decide crimes and punishments that exist in the setting. Whether they apply to a given jurisdiction should be decided in the sovereign powers or settlements sections, but the items themselves can be defined here. Which crimes result in a given punishment is determined by the locality, and one punishment can fit many crimes. You will likely invent more crimes than punishments as a result.

CRIMES

Crime Name: _____

Description: _____

_____

Crime Name: _____

Description: _____

_____

Crime Name: _____

Description: _____

_____

Crime Name: _____

Description: _____

_____

_____

Crime Name: _____

Description: _____

_____

_____

Crime Name: _____

Description: _____

_____

_____

Crime Name: _____

Description: _____

_____

_____

Crime Name: _____

Description: _____

_____

_____

Crime Name: _____

Description: _____

_____

_____

Crime Name: _____

Description: _____

_____

_____

Crime Name: _____

Description: _____

_____

_____

Crime Name: _____

Description: _____

_____

_____

Crime Name: _____

Description: _____

_____

_____

Crime Name: _____

Description: _____

_____

_____

Crime Name: _____

Description: _____

_____

_____

Crime Name: _____

Description: _____

_____

_____

Crime Name: _____

Description: _____

_____

_____

Crime Name: _____

Description: _____

_____

_____

Crime Name: _____

Description: _____

_____

_____

Crime Name: _____

Description: _____

_____

_____

Crime Name: _____

Description: _____

_____

_____

_____

Punishments

Create a list of punishments unique to the setting. Something basic like imprisonment can be assumed unless you want to rule it out, so it won't need an entry here, perhaps.

Punishment Name:
_____

Description:
_____

_____

_____

Punishment Name:
_____

Description:
_____

_____

_____

Punishment Name:
_____

Description:
_____

_____

_____

Punishment Name:
_____

Description:
_____

_____

_____

Punishment Name:
_____

Description:
_____

_____

_____

Punishment Name:
_____

Description:
_____

Punishment Name: _____

Description: _____

_____

Punishment Name: _____

Description: _____

_____

Punishment Name: _____

Description: _____

_____

Punishment Name: _____

Description: _____

_____

Punishment Name: _____

Description: _____

_____

_____

EDUCATION SYSTEMS

In this section, you will decide what education systems are possible. In your sovereign powers and settlements, you will then indicate which ones exist.

SYSTEM 1

What is the name of this system?

_____

What types of opportunities exist? Basic education, special education (like college or tech schools), or apprenticeships?

_____

_____

_____

_____

What sort of curriculum exists? Don't create an entire course of study if not needed, but what subjects are taught? What languages must be understood and to what Earth grade level? Are there unique (and feared) tests?

_____

_____

_____

_____

_____

_____

_____

_____

_____

_____

Do students live at home, in boarding school, with their master if an apprentice? For how long? Weekdays, a semester, a school year, or until graduation?

_____

_____

_____

Are libraries, labs, and more on campus, offsite, or off world? What kinds are available and needed?

_____

_____

_____

Is this a public school and there's no cost? An apprenticeship might mean menial tasks. Can students work if their family can't pay? Is a period of service required after graduation?

_____

_____

_____

_____

_____

_____

STUDENT REQUIREMENTS

At what age must students enroll and when can they leave or graduate?

_____

_____

_____

_____

_____

Are genders treated equally? Are classes coed? Dorms? Bathrooms?

_____

_____

_____

_____

_____

_____

Are all species allowed? Who is not and why? Are some favored?

_____

_____

_____

_____

_____

Are there any famous past or present students?

_____

_____

_____

SYSTEM 2

What is the name of this system?

_____

What types of opportunities exist? Basic education, special education (like college or tech schools), or apprenticeships?

_____

_____

_____

_____

_____

_____

What sort of curriculum exists? Don't create an entire course of study if not needed, but what subjects are taught? What languages must be understood and to what Earth grade level? Are there unique (and feared) tests?

_____

_____

_____

_____

_____

_____

_____

_____

_____

Do students live at home, in boarding school, with their master if an apprentice? For how long? Weekdays, a semester, a school year, or until graduation?

_____

_____

_____

_____

Are libraries, labs, and more on campus, offsite, or off world? What kinds are available and needed?

_____

_____

_____

Is this a public school and there's no cost? An apprenticeship might mean menial tasks. Can students work if their family can't pay? Is a period of service required after graduation?

_____

_____

_____

_____

_____

_____

_____

_____

STUDENT REQUIREMENTS

At what age must students enroll and when can they leave or graduate?

_____

_____

_____

_____

_____

Are genders treated equally? Are classes coed? Dorms? Bathrooms?

_____

_____

_____

_____

_____

Are all species allowed? Who is not and why? Are some favored?

_____

_____

_____

_____

_____

Are there any famous past or present students?

_____

_____

_____

ABOUT THE AUTHOR

Randy Ellefson has written fantasy fiction since his teens and is an avid world builder, having spent three decades creating Llurien, which has its own website. He has a Bachelor of Music in classical guitar but has always been more of a rocker, having released several albums and earned endorsements from music companies. He's a professional software developer and runs a consulting firm in the Washington D.C. suburbs. He loves spending time with his son and daughter when not writing, making music, or playing golf.

Connect with me online

http://www.RandyEllefson.com
http://twitter.com/RandyEllefson
http://facebook.com/RandyEllefsonAuthor

If you like this book, please help others enjoy it.

Lend it. Please share this book with others.
Recommend it. Please recommend it to friends, family, reader groups, and discussion boards
Review it. Please review the book at Goodreads and the vendor where you bought it.

JOIN THE RANDY ELLEFSON NEWSLETTER!

Subscribers receive discounts, exclusive bonus scenes, and the latest promotions and updates! A FREE digital copy of *The Ever Fiend (Talon Stormbringer)* is immediately sent to new subscribers!

www.ficiton.randyellefson.com/newsletter

Randy Ellefson Books

Talon Stormbringer

Talon is a sword-wielding adventurer who has been a thief, pirate, knight, king, and more in his far-ranging life.

The Ever Fiend
The Screaming Moragul

www.fiction.randyellefson.com/talonstormbringer

The Dragon Gate Series

Four unqualified Earth friends are magically summoned to complete quests on other worlds, unless they break the cycle – or die trying.

Volume 1: *The Dragon Gate*
Volume 2: *The Light Bringer*
Volume 3: *The Silver-Tongued Rogue*
Volume 4: *The Dragon Slayer*
Volume 5: *The Majestic Magus*

www.fiction.randyellefson.com/dragon-gate-series/

The Art of World Building

This is a multi-volume guide for authors, screenwriters, gamers, and hobbyists to build more immersive, believable worlds fans will love.

Volume 1: *Creating Life*
Volume 2: *Creating Places*
Volume 3: *Cultures and Beyond*
Volume 4: *Creating Life: The Podcast Transcripts*
Volume 5: *Creating Places: The Podcast Transcripts*
Volume 6: *Cultures and Beyond: The Podcast Transcripts*
185 Tips on World Building
The Complete Art of World Building
The Art of the World Building Workbook: Fantasy Edition
The Art of the World Building Workbook: Sci-Fi Edition

Visit www.artofworldbuilding.com for details.

Randy Ellefson Music

Instrumental Guitar

Randy has released three albums of hard rock/metal instrumentals, one classical guitar album, and an all-acoustic album. Visit http://www.music.randyellefson.com for more information, streaming media, videos, and free mp3s.

2004: The Firebard
2007: Some Things Are Better Left Unsaid
2010: Serenade of Strings
2010: The Lost Art
2013: Now Weaponized!
2014: The Firebard (re-release)

Printed in Great Britain
by Amazon